T0110274

Epigraph

Vaagartha viva sampraktau, vaagartha prati pattaye,
Jagatah pitarau vande, Parvati Parameswarau.

Let the words and their meaning be as inseparable as the Parents of this Universe—Parvati and Parameswara.

SAFFRON GRASS

In pursuit of our glorious past

SUDHIR REDDY REBALA

PARTRIDGE
A Penguin Random House Company

Copyright © 2014 by Sudhir Reddy Rebala.

ISBN: Softcover   978-1-4828-1766-9
             Ebook   978-1-4828-1765-2

The copyright for individual stories vests with the authors

To order additional copies of this book, contact
Partridge India
000 800 10062 62
www.partridgepublishing.com/india
orders.india@partridgepublishing.com

Dedicated To My Beloved Dad
Sudhakar Reddy who watches over
Me eternally from heavens above and
Lord Shiva who takes good care of him.

Preface

No matter which country you belong to, you have a part of Indian legacy in you. This book will make you think and explore. It will change your views about the world in general and India in particular. Some startling revelations made in this book might make you uncomfortable.

What is manifest is known and what is not manifest is unknown. The unknown is also the part of reality as much as the known. Therefore what is unknown need not necessarily be false. Science is not a static subject, but an evolving one. The day Science stops denying a possibility of something, that day Science is dead.

I have written this story to throw light on some facts. The fiction part is quite evident. But for those who would love to argue with me, claiming that most of what I had written is simple fiction, I urge them to conduct their own research and arrive at the truth.

It is my ardent desire that this book be read by every Indian, especially those who think poorly about India and its past.

This is a good book to be read by anyone who wants to know about India, its ancient history and how and how this great country had influenced human civilizations throughout the world thousands of years ago.

I have taken great care to establish a common thread among all the religions. Rig Veda says 'Truth is one, but the sages speak of it by many names.' All religions aim at making humans better. Narrow minded religious leaders have misinterpreted the faiths. Those who encourage violence and mayhem in the name of God and religion are doing a great disservice to the Humanity.

If I am able to create a positive understanding of the facts mentioned in this book in the minds of the readers, I would consider myself and my effort of some decent worth.

-Sudhir Reddy Rebala

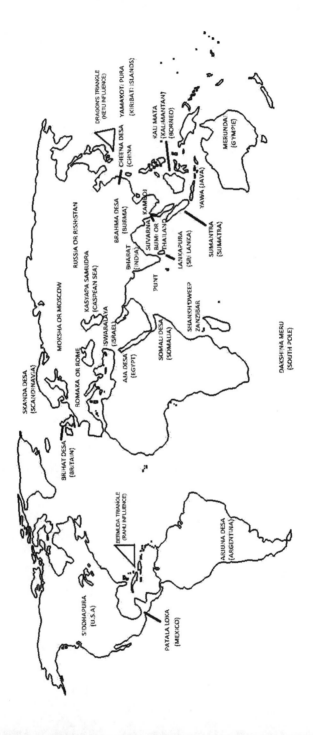

CHAPTER: ONE

Silence knows no language. It has no emotion. It does not convey any meaning and does not expend any energy. It is the primal note punctuated by the sounds of nature and the organic life, until Man decided otherwise.

The ringtone on his cell phone reflected his devout nature. The chaste voice of Paul McCartney filled the room with 'When I find myself in times of trouble Mother Mary comes to me, speaking words of wisdom, let it be . . .' Professor Ramos Ramirez reached for the phone. It took a few moments for the reality to sink in into this erudite scholar on history and anthropology.

'I will be down in ten minutes' he said with an air of authority and slid up the phone.

He went to the washroom and sprinkled cold water on his face. Looking at mirror he reckoned that plain flat mirrors

1

reflect the truth. Man's quest for unanswered questions made him a voyager, an explorer and a discoverer.

Prof. Ramos ate a quick meal made out of Quinoa, rated as the best food on the planet with highest protein content and nutrients. This food of the Gods helps build muscle and cuts down fat. This gluten-free food that has proven to be ideal for diabetics due to its low-glycemic index, has been cultivated and eaten by the Mexicans and Incas for thousands of years. In his two decades of exploration, he had seen many sites that lay in ruins. They told their stories through burnt skeletons, destroyed temples, uprooted settlements and signs of genocides or natural calamities. The deeper he and his team explored the Mexican jungles the more sites of Mayan civilization they found.

The team that waited for him outside his apartment consisted of couple of his assistants and four construction workers. The large grey Toyota SUV looked very unassuming at the street side. Ramos being a tall man preferred to sit on the front seat beside the driver. He replied the greetings with equal enthusiasm.

Their journey would take them deep into the jungles of Mexico. The SUV has been customized to handle all types of off-road terrain. An ingenuous automotive engineer had fitted an additional overhead fuel tank to the car to facilitate long drives.

Closing his eyes for a prayer, Ramos slowly slipped into a deep slumber. Suddenly he was pushed to the front only to be halted by the seat belt. The car had come to a screeching halt. About a dozen hyenas stood in front of them. They looked menacingly at the vehicle grunting with rage. Professor Ramos asked the driver to switch on the headlights and keep driving. At that very moment all the hyenas parted to either side as if they were paying their respect to their chief.

They had never seen such a huge hyena in their lifetime. Before they realize what was happening, it charged towards the van and as the driver let loose the clutch it hit the animal with a big thud and ran over it.

'Keep driving fast . . . faster' the professor yelled. A splatter of blood on the windscreen started coagulating. They were approaching the ancient ruin site of Uxul, which was excavated in 1934. Couple of years ago, the team found a Royal palace and two large dried man-made lakes. A week ago the professor had inadvertently stumbled upon a secret passage in one of the royal chambers.

He had deployed a team of four construction workers and his deputy to clean the passage and make it more habitable. His deputy had called the Professor couple of days ago to inform him that he found a small chamber at the end of the tunnel that lead to the deep jungles. The door of the chamber had many intricate drawings of snakes and it was tightly sealed.

The professor had asked him to carefully break the door and report. That was the last communication from either side. The past 24 hours have been very tough on the Professor. The area was out of cell phone coverage and there was no response from the satellite phone handset.

He had requested an acquaintance at a nearby town to visit the site and report. There has been no communication from him either. This put the professor in a tense mood. The attack of the hyena was a bad omen. He clutched on to his chain locket touching his heart and opened it looking at the image of Mother Mary and Jesus Christ.

They had almost approached the site when the driver slammed his brakes. Right ahead of them laid a dead body. He jumped out to take a closer look. The body was severely mutilated and most of the flesh was missing. The eyes were gouged out and the body was almost naked. The body belonged to that of the acquaintance that had gone to the site to check on the team.

Professor Ramos mechanically went to the vehicle and opened his bag and grabbed his revolver. The workers carried the body and dumped it the boot and they reached the site. The place looked desolate. They walked past the entrance and proceeded straight to the tunnel. Four large snakes were hissing on the ground at the entrance. Killing them was an easy task for the workers. The professor understood that the acquaintance had died due to the snake bite. Switching on the flash lights and large lamps they slowly entered the tunnel.

They found dead bodies of the construction workers and his deputy. Their faces were charred by some chemical substance. The stench was unbearable and nauseating. He heard the grunt again. The professor reached for the revolver and in a flash of the moment he fired at two ferocious demonic looking hyenas that charged towards him. He approached the chamber door. The walls and floor were splashed with an acidic substance. Inside the chamber was an idol of a person that resembled that of the Prince. The door had many drawings inscribed on it. The professor found it amusing as the inscriptions and images had Hindu symbols.

A large metal box was found beneath the idol. The workers entered the chamber and carefully removed the idol. The earth shook for a few moments and they heard lightning and sound of rain. They brought the trunk out and broke it open. Immediately, a dozen darts flew in all the directions. They hit the workers and the supervisor and they collapsed instantly. The professor and his deputy had a narrow escape. It took a few moments for them to check on the fallen colleagues. They were dead.

Fear gripped both of them. The deputy professor started shivering. Fear, some say is a useful emotion that stimulates most of the living beings into either into a defensive or an offensive manner. It also precludes him from venturing into dangerous situations. The Professor moved towards the box and looked inside.

He found another metal box smaller in size inside the main box. He opened it. Inside he found a casket and a metal plank and an object as large as a rugby football. He replaced the lid and with the help of the deputy brought it out. They walked towards the vehicle. It was pouring and the lightning constantly bombarded the area. The dark clouds had blocked the sunlight.

The driver's body lay motionless at the wheel. His tongue had protruded and a large snake was coiling around his neck. The professor pulled down his body and the snake uncoiled and moved away from him.

CHAPTER: TWO

The distinct addictive aroma that wafted through the air was unmistakably that of the brewing South Indian Robusta Filter Coffee. Ravi, in his jeans and Che Guevara tee shirt, religiously stood at the serving counter to savor its invigorating flavor. The Southern Indian Metropolis of Chennai runs on Filter Coffee. It is a part of the city's tradition. Making Coffee is considered an art here. Every year, the Coffee shop chains are ranked on the quality of Filter Coffee they serve. For Ravi and his friends, this Coffee shop on Marina beach, the longest beach in India, doubled up as a venue for discussing and debating every weekend.

Beside him stood a tall muscular person, with disheveled hair and unshaven beard. His name is Vikram Reddy. Friends called him Vicky. Vicky worked as a professor. He was commissioned by the University of Madras, to develop a new branch that combined Noetic science,

Religion, Philosophy, History and Anthropology. Ravi on the contrary, ran a primary school and held orthodox and anti-capitalistic, communist views. The other person who completed the trio is Ram whose eyes and mind were lost focusing on the blue expanse of Bay of Bengal. He owns one of the largest bookstores in the city. He is a staunch Hindu and indulges in praying for about 4 hours daily.

Vicky had invited them for an impromptu celebration as he was invited by the Rixton University in the United States. He obtained the Visa that day. In fact, he wanted to have more than just coffee and so he had invited them to come over to KFC, his favorite joint. 'Kentucky Fried Chicken, especially the Original Recipe made perfect by Colonel Sanders with eleven secret ingredients, is the best food on the planet', Vicky advertised often for the culinary colonel. Alas! The Original Recipe was no longer available in India and Vicky was eager to taste it on his impending trip to the United States.

Chennai is a city with the largest population of vegetarians in the world and Ram was a hardcore Vegetarian. So, Vicky had to give in and he agreed to meet at their default Coffee Shop.

Along with genuine friendship, shameless teasing and sharing jokes, this group played an extremely dangerous sport, which is barely legal and is punishable by law. Every Saturday night, they would get their motor cycles to race from the entrance of Chennai International Airport to

St. Thomas Mount, the place where Saint Thomas, the apostle of Christ was murdered 2,000 years ago.

Chennai city has the largest number of Motorcycles in the world and the art of motorcycling on lightweight 100 CC bikes is a favorite sport of the city, this in spite of the city being dubbed as the next largest hub of Car manufacturing and a competing IT hub. What was once a small trading post has now expanded into a major city in South Eastern India. The British made this city, known better as Madras—named after a family having surname 'Madre'—its headquarters to rule over Southern India. The city was later renamed as 'Chennai', after a Telugu Chieftain, Chennappa Nayakudu.

The sultry and humid climate of the city makes air-conditioning a necessity. The British who colonized India perished in dozens during Summer time in this city. The slow growth of infrastructure and amenities never dampen the spirit its citizens as they take everything in their stride, so much so, these racing trio on road was a mere 'inconvenience'.

Vicky never won a bike race in his life. He always got nervous when he had to bend the machine beyond a certain degree. Five days earlier, he lost the race by 54 seconds.

'So, you are visiting your Father land, you pseudo Indian!' Ravi teased him, sipping Coffee.

'Ravi, your comment is unfair. I adore the United States no doubt. But, my roots will always be in India. I love India too' replied Vicky sipping Pepsi off the can.

'You cannot possibly love two countries equally at the same time'

'Is it so difficult?'

'I know it is futile to make efforts to change your mind. I do not know why you are so fascinated by that country! You must understand and accept certain facts about America,' Ravi started his anti-American propaganda.

'The country you adore so much, the United States is on its path to self-destruction. Did you read the report by The National Security Council? It predicted that the American century will come to an end by 2025. That country survives on debt adding more than a trillion dollars every year'

'I know about that report Ravi. But don't forget the American resilience. They are champions and they can and they will bounce back'

'Money matters apart, that country kills its own people. In the 1960s, General Lyman Lemnitzer tried to execute a sinister plot called Operation Northwoods, to conduct Terrorist strikes on the US civilians and push the blame on Fidel Castro and use that as an excuse to invade Cuba. But, it did not take off, due to the refusal from

John. F. Kennedy. So, the right wing military generals implemented that plan on a later date and sank their own ship and compelled the US Administration to get into Vietnam misadventure'

'They are just rumors' Vicky protested.

'Everything about America is wrong. Let me prove it to you' Ravi grabbed the can of Pepsi from Vicky and placed it on the table. The other two friends watched silently.

'What do you read on the tin Vicky?'

'Pepsi'

'And what is this circle with wavy blue and red?'

'It signifies the world. Pepsi says that it is the symbol for Generation Next'

'Good. Now read this' Ravi tilted the can upside down.

It read iSdEd and there was the circle before the words.

'Is ded' Vicky spelt it out

So, Pepsi says 'The Generation Next is Dead. You should not be drinking this every day. You and your American corporations are enslaving people around the world'

'You are paranoid Ravi. If Pepsi was harmful, how do you think it survived so long? It is a fine drink. I sincerely suggest you start drinking it too. In fact you can make great Mock-tails with it.' argued Vicky.

Ram intervened 'Vicky, why are you going to the U.S?. My intuition says this trip will change your life'

'There has been some discovery in Mexico Ram. Archeologists unearthed some objects believed to have some Hindu religious connotations and I am being called to take a look at it.'

Ram gazed at the Sea and said 'The world will someday learn that our ancestors went around the world and formed the bedrock for other cultures and civilizations or strongly influenced them.'

'There he goes again' Ravi lifted his hands up and sipped his coffee.

'You never agree with me. Do you know that the name 'America' has its origins from the world 'Amara Loka', which in Sanskrit meant 'The Land of Gods'

'Oh. Come on. Spare me tonight. It was named after Amerigo Vespucci, an Italian explorer'. Vicky said correcting his friend.

Ram was defiant 'No Vicky, Amerigo was just a chandler under Columbus. The original inhabitants of the United

States were the Hindus from India. The United States was called as 'Siddha pura' those days. Grand Canyon has massive temples of Shiva, Vishnu and others Hindu deities constructed tens of thousands of years ago rising above the vast expanse of the Canyon. There is a large inscription of Om in Sanskrit carved on the mountains.'

Ravi put both his index fingers on his forehead and raised his voice 'Ram, you are watching too much of religious channels man. No wonder, you don't even have a steady girlfriend. And this nonsense theory of yours is not even worth a tissue paper'

Ignoring Ravi's provocation, Ram continued 'Britain was in fact 'Bruhat desa'. Russia was 'Rishistan', the land of Rishis or Seers, who meditated and lead a pious life. The city of Moscow is considered to have originated from the word 'Moksha' or the salvation. When river Saraswati dried up, a tribe from Kashmir, by name 'Kalatoyas' or Celts migrated to Danube River that covers 12 European counties. The river got its name from Danu, wife of Sage Kashyap, who gave birth to a demonic race called the Danavas. Sage Kashyap's disciples settled around the Caspean Sea and named the water body after him. Kashmir in India is another region that derived the name from Sage Kashyap. One Indo-European priestly clan, 'Sharmas' or 'Sharmans' migrated to teach and civilize and were later called 'Germans'. They carried many cultural traits of Aryans with them, the bad name it wrought because of that megalomaniac, Adolf Hitler.

The warrior Jat tribe from Haryana, India had migrated to Scandinavia, named after the Warrior Hindu God Skanda, who is the son of Hindu God Shiva. In Kurukshetra, where the major battle occurred circa 5,000 years ago, a temple for Skanda was built, which even today is anointed with oil every day. Historians agree that this tribe formed Jat land or Jutland. They named their capital as Asigarh which is also the name of a city in Haryana. They had even constructed a temple dedicated to Ahilya, wife of a Sage.'

'Ram, I don't entirely deny what you are saying. But, unless there is concrete evidence, I cannot accept these things' Vicky clarified. Diverting the discussion, Vicky continued 'Okay guys, what you want from the U.S.?'

'Get me the books 'Nine Hours to Rama' and 'Unarmed Victory' They are banned in India'

'Okay Ram, I will break the law for you' Vicky said.

'But why are those books banned in India?' asked Ravi asked.

'The book 'Nine Hours to Rama' is based on the life of Nathuram Godse, who killed Gandhi. The book defends him a certain way and exposes the careless security lapses. The book 'Unarmed Victory' is banned as it talks about why India lost the Sino-India war' replied Ram.

Vicky went home and changed into his pajamas. He brushed his teeth and looked at himself in the mirror. He noticed a few dried up blood spots at the edge of his nose. He washed them away. For the past few days, he has been experiencing blood oozing from his nose. He did not want to scare his parents, but visited a doctor who prescribed some tests. The results will be due in a week, but Vicky would be out of the country by then.

CHAPTER: THREE

It all started couple of years back. He had just finished a thesis describing why Tantra must be made a part of Noetic Science. The subject of Noetic Science is young. It has been nurtured and developed by the Astronaut Edgar Mitchell and Paul Temple in the state of California in the United States since 1973. Noetic Science focused on the power and potential of human psychic powers and the power of conscious and sub-conscious mind. It delves into the areas of meditation, yoga, spontaneous remission and psycho-kenesis.

Vicky showed tremendous interest in this subject since his school days. He went into deep meditation during weekends sometimes. His heightened consciousness helped him and also troubled him. On a given day he would receive a sudden negative feeling that he might be involved in a road accident and he would drive carefully on that particular day.

This clairvoyant prognosis also makes him vulnerable and sensitive to negative fields of energy. Places that have concentrated negative or evil force instantly made him sick.

However, he was able to understand, control and subjugate this weakness by learning the dynamics of energy fields at sub-conscious level and the methodology to be followed to use the mental energy to control the physical domain. This happened to him in Kerala, a beautiful state in Southern India.

In Kerala, a retired senior police officer T.P. Sundar Rajan had gone to the court seeking intervention on the administration of a temple in Kerala state. The temple going by the name Ananta Padmanabha Swami temple had been under the patronage of Travancore kings.

The court directed that an exhaustive inventory list be made of all the temple assets and it constituted a panel of seven members lead by Sundar Rajan, the petitioner. The temple has six vaults and four of the vaults were occasionally opened and shut. But, the two main vaults were not opened as the priests had warned of huge calamities particularly if the second vault was to be breached.

This lead to a war of words and the panel had sought the advice of seers and also the scientific community. Vicky was asked to give his opinion. He had stayed in Tiruvanantapuram for many weeks. He met with the holy men, the priests and he studied the inscriptions on the doors and other planks. The first vault was opened and Sundar Rajan had incurred the wrath of the occult curse. He died suddenly a few months later.

This was Vicky's first real life encounter with the effect of Tantra occult. What had been written in theory is now emerging out to be of factual significance. He had an opportunity to understand and appreciate the occultist's viewpoint.

After a thorough analysis, Vicky agreed with the assessment of the holy men that the second vault must remain closed. He had deciphered the ominous writing and the symbols on the doors of the second vault. It has clear depiction of the Snake guard or Nag Bandh. He spent many months learning the secrets of sacred ritual called the Tantra under the powerful guidance of Unni Krishnan, a truly pious man who lived in a small hermitage.

A few days later, he submitted his report concurring with the priests. He returned to Madras University and continued his work. He shared his findings with the Noetic Science community. One day he received a call from Rixton University. IONS had suggested that Vicky was the most suitable one to deal with the subject at hand.

CHAPTER: FOUR

Every step he took was a burden. The soft snow beneath his feet was getting increasingly deeper. Vicky stood still and looked around. The rising Moon was chasing the setting Sun. All he could hear was the sound of ghastly wind piping through the hills and his own unabated breath. If he did not make it to his destination before the night fall, he would suffer from exhaustion, frost bite and possibly death.

When Man loses hope on everything else, his faith in God gets stronger. When Mind sees no alternative, it ceases all other thoughts, all other emotions, all other distractions and all the scattered energies of mind assimilate into a pointed ray of light, throwing up a cry of the soul to the Divine.

Walking a few steps with silent prayer, he saw a cave with light emanating from it. His excitement worked as an antidote to the exhaustion. As he approached the cave, he heard a reverberating sound of 'Aum'. In the cave, he saw a man sitting in meditative posture. This person had a long beard and his body was lean and firm. There was a glow around his body, especially from the top of his head. Vicky stood spell bound. The person opened his eyes that shone like diamonds. Then, he glanced at the walls of the cave and the entire cave lit up a hundred lamps. He turned to Vicky and said 'You have found me at last'.

A sharp hit made Vicky's head go reeling. When he opened his eyes, all he saw was panic. He found himself on a commercial passenger Jet of Emirates Airways. It took him a few moments to realize that he has been dreaming. The captain was speaking rapidly in Arabic and the flight stewardess was busily pulling away the service trays from the aisle. The air packets over the Atlantic Ocean were notoriously large shaking up the large A380 aircraft like a toy.

He realized the shameful posture of occupying the entire middle column of seats in the economy class making it into a luxurious bed that even first class passengers should envy. This suited well especially for Vicky as he was 6'3" tall.

He quickly sat up and fastened his seat belt. He felt so exhausted and famished. But, he knew there was hardly any chance of the red capped girls coming with the food trays anytime soon.

The stewardesses were busy elsewhere and no one had the chance to obstruct him to walk to the water closet. The moment he entered the toilet, he read a warning sign asking the passengers not to soil the toilet and to keep it dry. He was amused to find this message written in Telugu, his native tongue, on the second line, very next to Arabic. Was this a sign of Telugu people traveling a lot or was it a sign that Telugu people soiled the toilets a lot? It was a compliment and an insult rolled into one.

The entire airline industry has gone on penny pinching cost cutting drive. As victims of the global recession, the airline industry could not afford to pamper its passengers with frills as they used to once upon a time. Now, meals were conveniently served not based on the biological clock, but based on the longitude on which the aircraft was flying. He drew comfort from the snacks that Emirates served between the meals. Situation was so bad that reputed airliner such as British Airways stopped serving their famous sandwiches in their Trans-European routes.

After gorging on the hot and cold meal, Vicky ruminated on the weird dream he had. He was visiting the United States to assist Professor Chris Conrad of the Rixton University to decipher an object and the writing on a plank that were found in the excavations in Mexico. Being one of the very few persons in the specific branch of knowledge which Vicky had pioneered, he was the clear choice of Prof. Chris to help unravel the mystery.

He had watched all there was to watch on the entertainment service. Seated across the aisle was an Indian family. The father was explaining his Son about how the aircraft flies. He was explaining how brilliant the Americans were in conjuring up the science of flying. Vicky grinned when he heard that.

'Am I saying something wrong here?' inquired the Dad.

'Not entirely sir. But a few parts . . .'

'Which part?'

'Most of us think that the Americans had originally designed the aircraft. Very few of us are aware that the design and the principles of flying were written in a book called 'Vimana Sastra' written by Sage Bharadwaja, tens of thousands of years ago'.

'So, do you mean to say that the Wright Brothers copied the technology from our ancient scriptures? This sounds crazy. If we knew how to fly, why did we not build the aircrafts'

'Sir, I can't answer your question. But, I can tell you definitely that these principles of making the aircraft were known to us since ancient times. For some unknown reason, we did not materialize them. For example, Pythagoras copied his principle from ancient Indian Maths text written by Bhaskara. It is also not a common knowledge that Picasso copied his style from the cave paintings of Adivasis of Bihar. These paintings were done thousands of years ago'

'Quite interesting'

'There are many such instances. But, I don't want to spoil your fun. I will go back to my sleep'

Vicky closed his eyes. He could not sleep. His thoughts were around the dream. Was it a good omen or a bad omen? Why was he thinking of omens? He was supposed to be scientist and not an orthodox believer. Perhaps, it was a side effect of having too much of religion in his mind.

It was afternoon and it was pouring out like hell and heaven put together in downtown New York. Vicky wanted to view the city. But his plane just landed off on JFK International Airport without much of a picture show. For Vicky, rain always brought good luck.

John F Kennedy International Airport's Terminal 4 is the favorite of seasoned travelers as it has the most modern facilities. JFK Airport employed 35,000 people and its annual revenue of more than US $ 30 Billion, is sufficient to run many countries.

He had asked the Professor not to send anyone to the airport to pick him up, as he wanted to be left alone through the weekend to savor the Big Apple all by himself. He had booked his room at the Plaza Hotel, because it gave him the best sight of the city. He hopped into a taxi and looked excitedly out through the glass window.

After a while, he struck a conversation with the taxi driver. He saw his name sounded Russian, Vladimir Kirnakov.

'So are you from Russia?'

'No Ukraine. My parents were born there. I am born here'.

'Ever been to Ukraine?' asked Vicky.

'Yes. To Kiev, mother of all cities and the oldest one in the erstwhile USSR'

'No. Kiev was believed to be the oldest, until a few years ago. But, in fact, there was a civilization hundreds of years before Kiev was born. About 2,000 years ago, Hindus from India had migrated there and built a large temple of Vishnu. The place is Starya Maina village at Ulyanovsk on the banks of Volga River . . .'

'Are you from India?'

'Yes.'

'So, you are saying that Indians went to Russia, just as they arrived and settled all over America?' Vicky nodded silently. The number of Indians living in the United States had risen so sharply in the past decade, propelled by the Information Technology revolution, so much so that the

American President celebrated 'Diwali' the Indian festival of lights at the White House.

Vicky did not want to irk the Ukrainian pride anymore. So, he started out of the window, savoring the sights of the beautiful city. But, his memory pushed him to reflect on the conveniently-forgotten facts of ubiquity of Indian settlements around the world and the long lectures of his friend back home.

An hour later, he would be sleeping like a log on the luxurious bed of Plaza Hotel.

CHAPTER: FIVE

The name 'Big Apple' was attributed to New York City by one Edward Martin in his book 'The Wayfarer' in the year 1909 and the name caught on popularity in the 1970's. Many people believed the name had originated from a house of ill repute, in New York where there was a Madam by name 'Eve'. This fictitious account was disavowed and the actual origin of the name was established.

Also dubbed as the Financial Capital of the World, with one quarter of Gold bullion of the world housed down the Wall Street in the Federal Reserve Bank, the city is home to about 800,000 registered companies.

Although New Yorkers are aware that their city was the First capital city of the United States and that George Washington had taken the oath on the balcony of Federal hall in 1789, only a few are aware that Manhattan was purchased by a Dutch explorer Peter Minuit from the natives for trinkets worth $ 24 and that the city was originally named New Amsterdam. The Dutch built a wall to protect themselves from the attacking Indian tribes. The street famously came to be known as Wall Street. The city was renamed as New York after the Duke of York, the King's brother.

The skyscrapers that mushroomed on the island of Manhattan owe their presence to unique hard rock soil formation that occurred during the last ice age. The formation of Long island and the archipelago occurred around 10,000 years ago. Excavations revealed that the nomads moved out of this place when the glaciers retreated.

The Plaza and Warldorf-Astoria are the only hotels in New York that were granted the status of National Historic Landmark. Plaza Hotel charging 700 dollars a night for a room is one of the most sought after, by celebrities and dignitaries. Ironically, in 1985, Western countries met here and signed what has come to be known as 'The Plaza Accord' to bring down the value of the American Dollar.

Vicky had chosen this Hotel for its historical importance. Money was not the criterion, when he decided to reserve a room at this Hotel. He has been a pampered kid since his childhood. His Dad always kept his family in luxury in spite of his ups and downs in life.

Donald Trump had bought this property and sold it at half the price after a few years. It's the experience that counts. Now, the Hotel belonged to an Indian Business Group. He woke up when the Sun went down on the city at 7:00. His body clock was still crying for its morning South Indian Filter Coffee, which he usually drank reading three newspapers. After a quick shower he went right its basement food court to get a sandwich and coffee. It is one of the peculiarities of this luxury hotel to have a Food Court at the basement instead of a Gourmet restaurant.

He planned to take a walk down the Fifth Avenue and then catch a cab to the Times Square to spend rest of the evening on its Neon light soaked street. He was eager to get into the New York Subway, the only city rail in the world that ran round the clock. But, he decided to do that the following morning. As he got onto the walk, the city looked dream-like. The yellow taxi that originated in New York City thanks to its founder John Hertz who decided on the yellow color for its brightness, was ubiquitous. One of his friends back home had cautioned him about the Gypsy cabs.

Yellow color according to ancient Indian texts is the color of resistance. It freezes the onlooker's thought process and the mind gets focused on the object. This is the reason why Yellow color cars have the least number of accidents and the Grey and Silver cars meet with maximum number of accidents. Yellow color is also worn by people who participate in debates, as the color slows down the opponent's neuron-transmitters.

He had read enough about this great city. Now, he is experiencing it first-hand. He knew it was safe to visit the Times Square which was unthinkable a few years ago. It was Rudi Giuliani the famous city Mayor who cleaned up the mess, making New York City one of the safest cities in America.

As he hopped in the cab, he could not fail to notice the GPS navigator.

'Where to' asked the cabbie

'Times Square'

The car sped on the road. The cab driver a Bangladeshi was trying to be friendly. He spoke bad Hindi. So, Vicky tried to get back to English or American as the Americans call their language.

'So, do you have these navigators back in India?' he asked pointing to the device.

'Of course we do. In fact we are the originators of the term 'Navigator"

'What, I don't understand. Indians invented the Navigator?'

'Yes perhaps. With thousands of our scientists working here, that is a good guess. But what I meant was that the word 'Navigator' originates from the words 'Nav' and 'Gati' meaning the speed and direction of a vessel.'

'It is amazing sir. I never realized it.'

'Most of the words in English have their origins in Sanskrit through the intervening Latin. The word 'Mother' has its origins from 'Matr' and 'Father' from 'Pitr' you can see the resemblance in the numbers. 'Three' or 'Trinity' comes from 'Thri'. 'Septa' is from 'Sapta', 'Eight' is from 'Asta', and 'Deca' is from 'Dasa'. All the basic human expressions have their origins from Sanskrit language. It has highly evolved grammar and its syntax is exactly similar to the high end computer programing syntax.'

Then the conversation ran through the good places to get Asian food, the Basement Bangra dance and the places where one must be watchful in the city.

After coming back to the Hotel, Vicky made a phone call back home to Chennai to talk to his parents. His Dad shared some worldly advice. His mother insisted that Vicky stayed with her cousin brother who lived in New Jersey.

There was another reason why his parents were keen on having Vicky visit his Uncle's place. It's about his marriage. They wanted him meet Rachana, a young doctor whose family has been friends for many years. Vicky was not inclined to consider marriage particularly when he was on a mission the details of which are at the best sketchy.

CHAPTER: SIX

When he woke up the next morning, it was past nine in the morning. He was already late for his morning prayers. He had planned to visit many places that day. For Vicky, the entire world can wait, not his prayers. He quickly took a shower and put on fresh cloths.

He took out a cloth bag in which he had packed a rosary of 108 rosary beads called 'Rudrakshas'. These beads have tremendous positive energy in them. These rosary beads were believed, to be the tears of God Shiva by the Hindus. The rosaries used by the Buddhists also have 108 beads.

For ancient Indians, the number 108 bears great significance. They had calculated roughly that the distance between the Earth and Moon is 108 times the diameter of the Moon and the distance between the Earth and Sun is 108 times the diameters of Sun. The diameter of Sun is 108 times the diameter of the Earth. There are

12 houses in the astrological birth charts of the Hindus. These 12 houses have a combination of 9 planets giving 108 unique planetary positions. Their classical dance of Bharata Natyam has 108 unique hand and leg movements. According to the Ayurveda—the ancient science of healing—there are 108 places in a human body where the physical side meets the subtle body. There are 54 male alphabets and 54 female alphabets, totaling 108 in Sanskrit, the language spoken in ancient times in India and in which all the scriptures and mantras were written. In short, the Hindus held that the number 108 is a denominator that connects the Human to the Divine.

It was a habit he cultivated since his childhood. Closing his eyes, he went into deep meditation, chanting sacred powerful hymns one for every rosary bead that he touched and pushed with his fingers.

There is a very powerful temple in Southern India. This temple attracts somewhere between 50,000 to 100,000 devotees everyday and the money that is donated everyday by the devotees is two crores to ten crore rupees, which is roughly between half a million dollars to sometimes over 2 million dollars every day. This makes this temple, Tirumala the busiest and the richest temple on the Planet. Industrialists, Film stars, Sportspersons, Politicians and many Celebrities believe in the power and miracles that Lord Venkateswara or Balaji as he is popularly called, is capable of. Many experience instant answers to their prayers. The word 'Venkateswara' is the combination of

'Vem', 'Kata' and 'Eswara', which means 'Sin', 'Destroy' and 'God'—the God who destroys sins.

After praying to Balaji and other Hindu deities, Vicky meditated on Allah and Jesus for a few moments.

The true monks of his religion encouraged the followers to accept, respect and pray other Gods as well. Fortunately there is no dictum in the scriptures that forbid them to pray other deities. False priests and narrow minded false religious heads preached hatred against other religions. But thankfully for every such mistake, there are a hundred level headed Hindus like Vicky,

In fact the word 'Hinduism' is a misnomer as a religion. Hinduism is a way of life. The actual name of the religion is 'Sanatana Dharma' which means the 'Everlasting Religion'.

The practice of chanting a holy name is also found in other religions. In the Jewish Kabala, certain names and spells are denoted to bestow power to the chanter when it is chanted repeatedly for thousands of time. The word 'Kabala' comes from a sect of Hindu monks called 'Kapalikas', who intoxicated and chanted some holy names and they always carried a human skull 'Kapala' to imbibe occult powers.

In the beginning stages, many holy men of Kabala experimented chanting of certain names drugging themselves, sitting in a room with lit candles, trying to get an experience of God. Some succeeded and some died with brain hemorrhage.

That is why certain practices in Kabala are considered to be extremely dangerous and they must be practiced carefully and with full knowledge or guidance from learned Masters.

Like the learned Kabala practitioners, the Hindus also have understood the power of certain sounds that have the capability to generate tremendous positive energy. The collection of sounds when set in a proper syntax formed what is known as 'The Mantra'.

Vicky's friend Ram believes that the name 'Israel' comes from the Sanskrit word 'Iswaralaya' or 'The God's temple'. Jerusalem was named after 'Yadu Isa Alayam' or temple of Yadu God. Judaism was considered as a religion of the Yadus or Yadavas.

Similarly, much of the Middle-eastern countries were founded and ruled by Kings from India. Turvasu, a King from India formed the country 'Turkey'. Syria came from the Indian Sun god 'Surya'.

The positive divine energy was also codified in another way in form of a Geometrical notation. This Geometrical notation or the Circle of power is called 'The Yantra' which has become the store house of divine power.

The third aspect of Hindu worship is 'The Tantra'. In its simple form, Tantra is the act of worship or the physical movements of the devotee that propels the spiritual energy within and invokes the positive energy from the Gods.

The Mantra, Yantra and Tantra when used together with pure devotion are believed to make the person rise above Human limitations and elevate towards the Divinity.

It took Vicky an hour to complete his Puja or 'worship'. The word 'Hour' itself originated from ancient Indian astrological term, 'Hora'. The Hindus had calculated that a day and night consisted of 24 Horas thousands of years before the West started developing time concept.

Keeping his thoughts aside, he grabbed the New York Post, which incidentally is the oldest newspaper of America. He read the headlines and the article and resumed his tour of the great city.

It was unusually not as cold as it should be on that December morning. Vicky headed straight to the Rockefeller Center. Standing there to watch the people ice skating with the backdrop of all the Holiday decoration was a sight that is immensely memorable. Then he realized that it was Alicia Keyes who was singing live at the Rockefeller Center. Her soothing voice was wonderful to ears. What was more refreshing was the song she was singing 'The Empire State of Mind'.

Vicky at once felt an overwhelming emotion that this great city was inviting him with her arms wide open. Why not? Every person who loved this city felt this way.

Ellis Island, Statue of Liberty, the Wall Street and the famous bull at Merrill Lynch, Brooklyn Bridge and the Central park made him exhausted. He was amazed at the efficiency of the New York subway with its 468 stations, the largest Mass Transit system in the world. He savored the Krispy Kreme doughnuts at the Penn station. Oprah had recommended them as the world's best doughnuts. They simply melted in mouth.

As he walked towards his train, he was swept off his feet by the exquisite voice and music of a young lady playing a guitar. She had some boxes laid out on the floor and some dollars. He had read somewhere that the musicians performing under the Subway had to undergo rigorous audition screening. Some of them, he recollected, performed at the Carnegie Hall. He took out a ten dollar note out of his wallet and gave it to the girl.

Back in the Hotel, he sent a mail to Professor Chris about his arrival and his new cellphone number. Little did he realize that the following days would be the most tumultuous and eventful of his life.

CHAPTER: SEVEN

Circa 20,000 years ago. This period in the History of mankind as known to the Westerners, was when no human civilization existed in the Far East. Slowly, the Historians are coming to terms with increasingly convincing evidence of great civilizations in Asia and American continents.

Hindus had conquered most of the known world. Wherever they went, they taught the natives culture, science, religion and traditions. The degree of adaptation varied from civilization to civilization. The South East Asian countries had adopted Hinduism to a large extent. These kings of these territories married the princesses of mainland India. There were good trading and diplomatic relations. Throughout the World Hindu temples were built. Over the ages, they have been destroyed or converted into Buddhist monasteries. In the history of mankind, if there is a singular religion that had not gone on a war to protect itself, it's the Sanatana Religion which follows the Hindu way of life.

Indonesia was no different. The island of Java flourished with Hindu way of life. The Mayans prided themselves as the powerful nether world (Patala loka) inhabitants. Sri Lanka, Mexico, East Africa, some Indonesian islands and Europe were inhabited with tribes that followed Hinduism but had more inclination towards the occult.

The Sun looked as red as its viewer's eyes. That morning, Siva Varman was standing outside his court yard awaiting the news. Looking at the sky, he wondered how the Sun God had witnessed his ancestors migrating to the island of Yawa Dwipa thousands of years ago. Named after the staple barley or 'Yawa' that is grown on the island, this would famously be spelt as Jawa or Java of Indonesia, twenty millenniums later.

Siva Varman belonged to the Pasupata sect of Hindus who prayed to God Shiva. He was the Minister at the court of King Ravi Varman, his cousin brother. He had just completed the Rudra puja dedicated to his deity. This special worship is believed not only to appease the fierce form of God Shiva, but also to obtain fulfillment of 346 types of desires. The uniqueness of the worship lies in invoking Lord Shiva into oneself, before reciting the verses of Sri Rudram. This makes the worshipper a very powerful person.

In the ancient days, the power of a person was ascertained by his ability to control the minds and behavior of other people, the Nature and the events. This power was derived by the religious rites performed by that individual.

Siva Varman had sent an army to attack and kill a weird species which was half-human, half—chimpanzees, and which had dared to sail into the island from the western islands using bamboo rafts These animal like beings attacked the peace loving coastal populace and ate their food and destroyed their fields. There was no method to communicate with these beings.

Now, Siva Varman was eager to get the update. This very species his army was fighting would later come to be known as Hobbits and would pose a big mystery and debate thousands of years in future.

The modern western scholars today are extremely uncomfortable about admitting certain realities of History. One such fact is that one and a half million years ago, this region was ruled by a gigantic, powerful, demonic race which had mastered witchcraft and magic. The entire stretch of islands up to the South American continent shared the same culture.

Although most have perished, some of these giants yet remained but were restricted to deep jungle areas. But, when they visited the human settlements, they posed a problem. It is because they ate human flesh and were cannibals. No human could face them singularly. His capable army attacked and killed many such demons. So, he felt it was an easy job to chase away the half-human dwarfs.

Then, the messenger arrived

'Greetings, O Venerable Minister. I bring you good news'.

'Speak'

'Our army was able to vanquish the midgets. They were all killed and some were captured. The General wants to know what shall be done with them'.

'Ask the General to speak with me at the King's court. Dismissed'

Just as he set out to attend the court, a spy had sought his immediate audience. Usually, such meetings with the spies happened past midnight, so that the spy could leave the boundaries of the capital city before the dawn. It was dangerous to let the royal spies be identified by anyone in the palace or the capital. But, in times of exigency, the spies were required to pass the news without wasting a single moment. Mostly, at such times, the spies brought bad news.

At the King's court, there was a dance concert by 2 young ladies praising the greatness of King Ravi Varman. The singers praised the king to be equal to the Sun God. To this, the king proudly brushed his moustache with his right hand. The Good news of vanquishing the midgets had already been informed to the king by the General.

'What an idiot is he' thought Siva Varman to himself 'He wastes his time in such self-praise at the expense of taxes and time'.

After the celebrations, the King rose up and entered the inner chambers. Siva followed him.

'Your Royal highness, we are happily celebrating the event of vanquishing the midgets. We must bear in mind that this was an easy victory, for the midgets have little brains and were not civilized enough to have war craft'

The King interrupted 'Oh Siva. You always make me sad. Can't you praise the great achievement of our soldiers for at least one time?'

'Your Majesty. It is not my duty to please you. It is my duty to think only about your interests and your welfare.'

'Then, why are you so troubled?'

'It is because I just received an urgent message from our spy at Yamakotipura. He saw about 100 warships headed towards our kingdom and the ships were from Patala Loka'

'Are you sure they were warships? We had good relations with the Mayans, right? What makes them attack us now?'

'With due respect your highness. They believe that you have the Chintamani stone and I am sure they will attack us for that.'

45

'But, it was supposed to be a secret. How did they know?'

'The songwriters whom you have appointed for the purpose of singing your praise, have composed a song glorifying you as the owner of Chintamani and that gives you divine powers. The spies of Mayas have carried it their king and so he has set sail to wage a war against you'

'I am not a coward to sit here and let my kingdom be attacked by some Snake tribe. Call for the emergency military meeting. I will not rest until I vanquish these raiders. There shall be no more entertainment.'

Siva Varman knew how to touch on his cousin's nerve. Hilarious though the entire episode seemed, he was very well aware of the rumors his enemies constantly spread against his brother. The king of Yamakotipura (the modern day Kiribati islands) was one such enemy. He had urged his cousin several times to set on a voyage of conquest to defeat and annex these small kingdoms that created trouble. But, his cousin never heeded this advice. Now that he has seen the trouble approaching, he will shed all his eagerness for pleasure and put on his martial attire. In the battlefield, his cousin was a valiant warrior and he, Siva Varman was a brilliant strategist'.

The first thing he would do after this war was to banish the song writers from the service.

CHAPTER: EIGHT

Most of the English educated Indians find it difficult to appreciate the Hindu way of life. They eat out of their hands literally whatever the educational system has to offer them. It is difficult for them to reconcile science with Hinduism. When modern Science discovers something new that endorses what the ancient Hindus knew, they dismiss as a case of strong imagination on part of the ancient Hindus and as a matter of chance or coincidence that their theories had proven to be right.

According to the Hindu Surya Siddhanta written tens of thousands of years ago—when in fact the Humans did not evolve in Europe—the Mayan King Asura Maya ruled over Siddhapura or what is now known as the United States and Patala Loka or modern day Mexico during that period.

The Great epic of the Hindus, 'Ramayana' tells the story of how the evil Ravan abducted Sita, the wife of Ram, With the help of Cro-Magnon tribes depicted as monkeys, some of them who are powerful demi-gods such as Hanuman, Ram built a bridge across the ocean to Sri Lanka and crossed it with his troops and killed Ravan in the ensuing battle. Ram killed thousands of demons. He is said to have killed 40,000 demons in a matter of 39 minutes.

Ram is worshipped with deep devotion by many Hindus. But, it has become a fashion for some modern Hindu to question the credibility of Ramayana and the existence of humans such a long period ago. They tend to dismiss the Hindu Historical epics just as myths and not a reality.

Pitifully, they had to get the answers from the NASA scientists who confirmed that the bridge that was named as Adam Bridge between India and Sri Lanka was indeed a man-made structure built 1.7 million years ago, shockingly coinciding with the period of Ramayana.

Many civilizations flourished and vanished ever since in the archipelago. The geography itself had changed vastly. The land mass has moved away forming islands. Volcanoes erupted occasionally wiping out entire populations. Yet, the lifeline of culture, religion, art and commerce remained strong due to the advanced civilization of India that stretched from Saudi Arabia, Iran and Turkey to the West and Russia and Siberia to the North and Sri Lanka to the South and Americas towards the East.

Despite the rapidity with which the spy had carried the message, there was very less time, perhaps just one day or two to prepare for the war. The stakes were high on both sides. The spy had said that the Mayans have set sail with hundred ships. Would they have anchored at Yamakotipura or Kiribati islands to replenish their supplies? That was a sound assessment.

Twenty thousand years later, a brave Norwegian Thor Heyerdahl would sail from Peru to Tuamotu islands in his kon-tiki expedition to prove to the world that indeed civilizations and maritime existed.

Seated in the room were the Military General and other ministers. Two soldiers stretched the map on the table before them.

'Your majesty, the ships had to pass through the eastern island through a narrow trench. If we are able to block their advancement here . . . .' the General said pointing his finger on the map.

'That will result in a stalemate and a deadlock.' Siva Varman interrupted.

'But, this is the only way we can forestall the Mayan advancement'

'Our objective is not to forestall them, but to destroy them. By blocking them at this point, you are not only giving them the advantage of multi-flank positioning, but also providing them a curtain that can help them replenish supplies and troops. It also gives them the chance to flee and I do not want to see a single ship escape' Siva Varman roared.

'I agree. But, how do we do that?'

'We will attack them at Virya Jaya. The king there is in deep financial trouble. I can buy him out. He will pretend to seek friendship of the Mayans and invite them to be his guests. As a gesture of friendship, they will offer to give rations and also clean the ships. The cleaners will apply a thick coat of flammable oil on the strategic points and external layers of the ships.'

'How will that help us?'

'When most of the exposed parts of the ships are well oiled, setting arson becomes an easy job. All we would need is a bunch of sharp shooters. We will use the fire arrows and burn their ships. While the Mayans try to control the damage, we will surround them and use arrows from all the directions and kill them. Those who jump into the sea will be our prisoners.'

'Brilliant strategy I must admit' King Ravi Varman got up and placed his hand on Siva's shoulder. His cousin had the sharpest mind. He is capable of solving problems in matter of minutes.

'So, now let me rush to Virya Jaya before it is too late'.

As expected, the king of Virya Jaya accepted the deal and the Mayans fell into the trap. The Mayans made themselves to be sitting ducks to the Yawa army. Their defeat was so bad that they lost 98 ships and 2 of them made their way back. Thousands of them ended up as captives. Their king was killed. When this news reached the slain king's brother, he was furious. Before he could set sail to avenge his brother's death, one night his entire palace was burnt down with arrows that had their tips tied to a sticky burning tar coated cloth. By dawn, his mighty kingdom was reduced to ashes. He was made captive and he signed a humiliating accord with the invaders. Over a period of time, natural calamities and migrations made the civilization almost extinct.

Thousands of years later, historians discovered this as the first Mayan civilization, the edge of Indian Diaspora which would again resurface after 15,000 years.

CHAPTER: NINE

'Yes hello . . . Am I talking to Vikram Pandit?'

'You got the wrong Vikram. This is Vikram Reddy'

'Oh yeah. I am sorry Vikram. This is Jenny, I mean Jennifer Corning. I am on my way to pick you up. Just hang around in the lobby. Will be there in 20 minutes'

'Okay, I will inform the front desk and will wait . . . Hello . . . Are you there? Hmm' the girl had snapped the phone off on the other side.

'These nerds from India! Not only they have strange names, but they are so complicated. And I damn myself for having chosen this research field' cursed Jennifer Corning or Jenny for the lack of patience.

Jenny had a pensive disposition and she was irritated most of the time. She was clumsy in her own way. The first few minutes of exposure to her was enough to convince Vicky that he was dealing with a girl whose nervous system wanted to burst out of her body. First, she got his name wrong. Then, she had double parked her truck at the Hotel. Third, she did not have the patience to wait for Vicky to say some nice things to the Front desk girl. Fourth, she backed up the truck so fast that she almost hit a car. 'Damn you' was her instant reaction.

There was a reason that accentuated her nervousness. Things have not been normal in the past few days. She narrowly escaped death a week before, driving Prof. Ramos to the University from the airport. The Professor had brought with him a large wooden case that could not fit into the boot of the car. So, the professor opened the case and removed the smaller box. It accidentally fell on the ground and gave a crack. The black casing broke open and the contents of the box were exposed. He quietly placed the box in the boot and hopped in.

Scarcely had they left the airport when Jenny realized that all was not well with her automatic sedan. The instrumentation went awry and the car suddenly swirled horizontally. The car crashed against a wall. Air bags deployed and both of them were saved. But the Professor suffered serious injuries

Ambulance arrived and the Professor was hospitalized. He was safe but his injuries required complete bed rest. The

Professor thanked Mother Mary for saving his life once again.

While moving the box from the sedan lot of scotch tape was used to bind and hold the piece together. The next day Jenny and Professor Chris Conrad opened the box and it proved to be a Pandora 's Box as the hell broke loose quite literally.

The journey to New Jersey was an opportunity to get to know Jenny. She was a compulsive talker. She explained Vicky about the events. He was completely nonchalant.

After a while their conversation turned to more banal subjects.

'So, How was Lufthansa?' she asked.

'No. I did not fly Lufthansa. I flew with Emirates'

'Oh okay. Invariably, visitors from Madras err Chennai flew either with Lufthansa or the British Airways'.

'Yes. Maybe they like the name' Vicky chuckled.

'What name?'

'Lufthansa is a combination of 2 words, 'Luft' and 'Hansa'. Lufthansa stands for the Flying Hansa or the Flying Swan. Its Indian language, Sanskrit you see. Did you observe their logo? It's a flying Swan'

'Aah. I see . . . Interesting'

'Some of the guys from India are very strange you know. Last time there was this Professor Subbu. I can't spell his full name. Anyways, this guy lands in Newark and I had gone there to receive him as is my duty to chaperon every visiting professor. My professor Chris is a crazy guy. He thinks that it's a good gesture to receive people at the airport and drive them to the University quarters. I get so mad sometimes. Yeah. About this guy Subbu. He is a really funny character. He picked up a fight with the Customs officials and they had to detain him for intensive questioning before letting him off. It seems he had protested when the Customs officials did not permit him to bring in spices, wafers, sweet meat and all kinds of foodstuff he had brought from India. He had scolded the officer and insulted him saying all sorts of things about the Americans and their way of life. Those guys got all touchy and scanned his profile to see if it somehow linked with any American hating terrorist organizations'

'Whoa. You mean Prof. Subramaniam Sastry from Hyderabad?'

'Yes. The same guy, do you know him?'

'Of course'

'Oops. Did I bad mouth him?'

'No. It's okay.'

'This guy saw me first and asked where the driver was and he could not relish the fact that I can drive this truck. It was hot that day and I just wore shorts and a tee shirt. He was a weirdo I think. He kept his left hand covering his eyes from the side. I asked him what his problem was. Then pointing to my thighs, he said that I was naked. Jeez. I had never felt so naked until then'

Vicky burst out into laughter.

'It was not funny. I had to cover my thighs with National Geographic Magazine for Pete's sake. I also had lot of trouble understanding his dress. He wore a turban which he did not take off and then he had this checked bush coat and had a tie. He did not wear any trousers. He wrapped himself with a white cloth and wore boots . . . . he said he was hungry. It seems he had not eaten anything on the plane. I felt sorry for him and stopped by a MacDonald's joint and ordered fries and soda for him. He was a vegetarian you know. All he had to do was to sit, finish his meal and get out. Naah, he went to the counter and asked the guy there to show what oil they were using and he wanted to know if the same oil was used to fry chickens. No one understood what he was trying to say. It was his accent you see and he was talking too fast. I had to intervene and assure him . . .'

'Looks like you had a tough time with Professor Sastry'.

'Yes. He was kind of sweet in his own way. He had shown me his family album and his wife had sent me a Sari. I don't know how to wrap it around. I asked the professor if he could help. He screamed and ran out of the room . . . I still can't figure out why he did that and after that there was just a formal 'Bye'.'

Vicky burst out into another bout of laughter. It's been a long time since he had so much fun.

'Hey. What's so funny professor?'

'Nothing, I am sorry. I am just amused. By the way, if you take me out, I won't embarrass you.'

'Oh yeah, that is reassuring Professor'.

'You can call me Vicky'

'Thanks. It sounds easy'

Vicky was another victim to name cutting. The original names sounded very complicated to the westerners and shortening them helped. 'Swaminathan' became 'Sam', 'Sundaramoorthy' became 'Sunny', 'Krishnamoorthy' became 'Kris', 'Janardhan' became 'Joe' and now his name 'Vikram' has become 'Vicky'.

'So, Ms. Jennifer . . .'

'Just call me Jenny'.

'Okay. Jenny, what exactly do you study?'

'I am an assistant professor under Professor Chris and he had given me many assignments. He is hell bent upon proving that East has many hidden secrets unknown to the West and he digs deep into the ancient civilization to get answers to some unsettling questions. But he is not a religious man and does not believe in anything unscientific'

'I am amazed at Indian civilization. My specialization is the Ancient American Civilizations of the Mayans, Aztecs and the Incas.'

'This should be a very interesting topic to discuss'

'It will be an honor Vicky. Right now, we have a situation at hand'

At Rixton University, Professor Chris Conrad was very excited to see Vicky. After formal introduction to his colleagues, he took him to an adjoining building.

CHAPTER: TEN

The building was cordoned off and there were security personnel deployed all around the building. The professor and his team entered the building. It was completely dark inside. Just as Vicky began to wonder why, a huge wave of negative energy hit him.

It was not the first time that Vicky faced such strong negative force. His evolved stage of consciousness was sensitive to energy fields. But, this was too strong for him to counter. Someone switched on the mains and the entire lights kept flickering on and off continuously. A strong electromagnetic pulse was interfering with all the electrical systems in the building. When the casket was brought to the main building, it was opened from the small wooden box and kept on the table. Immediately, the lights flickered and the entire computer systems and cameras shut down. Engineers were called immediately but gave up as they could not figure out the reason.

They immediately realized that the object had correlation to the events. Professor instructed the box be moved to an adjoining building. All systems functioned normal again the moment the object left the place. The same phenomenon occurred in this building. Professor Chris had called some experts to explain the phenomenon. None but a scientist of Noetic Science explained that there was a field of deep negative energy and that it must be neutralized. He had suggested the name of Vicky for this purpose.

Vicky's memories of his time spent in learning at Padmanabha temple came rushing in. He knew what must be done to stop the dance of the dark power. But, it could not be practically implemented. He thought of a quick alternative. He turned to the Professor and told him that he needed two bottles of fresh drinking water and he requested the professor to leave him alone in the room for couple of hours.

The Professor wanted an explanation. Vicky replied that he would explain everything in detail later. Two bottles of water were arranged and he was left alone. Vicky sat on the floor in the center of the lobby and opened the lids of both the water bottles. With water from one of the bottles he completed the ablution procedure and he placed his palm on the open mouth of another bottle.

Then he began reciting the most potent energy neutralizing verse of the Hindu scriptures, The Maha Sudarsana Mantra 108 times. As he began the recitation, he began to see dark apparitions of fierce forms wailing and howling. Vicky took water from the bottle and sprinkled all over the place. A big scream of a demon reverberated through the air and the glasses of the building shattered. The Professor and others ran towards the building and switched on the mains. They lights worked this time. Vicky was visibly shaken.

After a few minutes later Vicky tried to explain about the negative energy field that was neutralized. He was now keen to see the object. Jenny brought him some Soda and then the Professor bent forward. 'This will blow your mind Vicky. Take a look at this' the professor placed a glass box before him. The broken contained a casket. He opened it and saw a golden plate badly tarnished and an object.

CHAPTER: ELEVEN

India is an enigma. Its past is a conundrum, complicated by literary accounts that are twisted to serve the interests of certain communities and sections. The history is shrouded with lies and incredible stories. There is hardly any text related to Hinduism that has not been subjected to manipulation and distortion.

Except for the Vedas, which are the four cardinal books of wisdom of ancient Hindus, and the Upanishads which are the treatise written on the essence of Vedas, everything else is suspected to have been altered. The 18 Puranas or legends portray their central theme on certain deity or a certain legend. Extreme liberties were taken by twisting these tales to promote certain agenda or ethics in India over thousands of years.

The tragedy of Hinduism lies in its inability to shrug off the falsehoods. Any person with certain knowledge of Sanskrit language and the holy texts can claim to be a Guru. The apocryphal stories they narrate to the uneducated and illiterate masses created dogmatic and orthodox rituals and customs.

The hunger to obtain super natural powers attracted the seeker to indulge in the wrong Tantric methods, or the Vama Tantra. This involved extremely vulgar activities involving women, wine and intoxicants and sometimes involved sitting on corpses. But, these activities were conducted by very few people, as they are dangerous and do not get religious sanction. Therefore, they are conducted in the cremation grounds by those who know the art of appeasing Gods and Goddesses at the lower strata of consciousness.

In remote villages, a few false God men cheat the gullible people saying that Gods desire sacrifice and the sacrifice involved animals and a fee to the self proclaimed God man. This unfortunate thinking has spread to other civilizations. The gradual deterioration of Hinduism was propelled by the popularity of Buddhism. But, Buddhism could not go beyond certain realizations. The Buddhists adopted the Vama Tantra and the wrong ways to obtain occult powers.

To save the Hindu religion and to bring the correct perspective to it, a great sage was born in the early 9th century A.D. His name was Adi Sankara. It was he who single handedly dismissed all the dogmatic rituals and cleaned up the religion. With this reformation,

Hinduism had taken a new vigor and helped people realize themselves and thus realize the divine. Disillusioned by this Renaissance of Hinduism, many Buddhists were panic-stricken and they had fallen prey to the lures of wrong Tantric methods.

Adi Sankara understood and explained in his works and deeds the principles of the Universe. This Universe is filled with energy. Matter is also a form of energy. The entire Universe is a mixture of neutral, positive energy and negative energy. The places where extreme positive energy manifested, negative forces tend to neutralize it. Adi Sankara showed the world that the cosmic energy called Shakti is the mother of all things that exists. She is the embodiment of all the good and the evil. The complement of Shakti is Shiva who is always in a state of complete stillness and selflessness. Adi Sankara was blessed with the power to manipulate this cosmic power delimiting the power as source of deities in temples in geometrical formations of Yantras. He was the one who literally spoke with the Gods.

All Hindu temples have an idol of God placed in the sanctum sanctorum or the inner temple. These idols were consecrated with holy waters and holy chants or the mantras, making them into powerhouses of positive god energy. This was an elaborate process consuming weeks of dedicated meditation and chanting by dozens of learned priests. When a Hindu visited a temple and prayed to certain deity, he can experience the power of that deity in the idol or statue.

Visiting temples also drove away the negative forces in a person. To maintain this positive energy at optimum levels, the priests perform special worships and rituals. Every temple in India has certain unique features. The sanctum sanctorum has a mound or a conical or pyramid structure on the top. The main gates of large temples are set in huge towers that rose above everything else in the vicinity. After completing the ritual of offering food to the deity with holy verses, the priests place morsels of rice mixed with pepper, salt and other condiments to appease the negative and evil forces and to curtail their movements to outwards of the temple and to preclude them from entering the positive energy field. Some even argue that the depiction of sexual acts in the sculptures outside the temples was for the appeasement of these satanic negative forces.

Unlike other faiths, Hinduism accepts the presence of negative and evil force and it also teaches how to keep such forces under control. The spiritually enlightened do not fear evil as they know that it also forms a part and parcel of the Universal Cosmic force.

Those Hindus who aspire to realize self and thus realize God focus their energies in meditation, Yoga and awakening of Kudalini, a power lying dormant in humans, which when awakened can accord great powers. It is believed that out of tens of millions of people, the desire to realize God germinates only in a few hundreds and out of these hundreds only one or two persons reach their goal.

One such person is Chandra. Born in a family of priests he was fortunate to have an opportunity to read the sacred texts at a very young age. To the dismay of his parents, he would spend most of his time in nearby woods in deep meditation. His elder brother often chided him for being lazy and for not taking up the responsibilities of household. As days passed by, his father turned intolerant to the behavior of young Chandra.

He was disappointed to see his poor performance at school. He explained the importance of education and financial independence to support spiritual pursuits.

'Promise me Chandra that you will focus your mind in gaining knowledge of the physical world. The education you receive in schools and colleges is to prepare you for higher realization. Remember that unless you are self-dependant economically when you grow up, you will never be able to evolve into a better human being.'

His growing passion for spirituality was constantly dampened by the financial problems his father faced. His father, a priest at a temple could barely make both ends meet. Chandra had an elder brother who went along with his father to conduct religious ceremonies and prayers. This made Chandra take up vocational job as a tutor for the children of a wealthy landlord.

Every day, he visited the large mansion to teach the young ones. The problem started when the landlord's eldest daughter started taking interest in Chandra. He tried his level best to keep her at a distance. One day when she expressed her love for him, Chandra went into a rage and slapped the girl. This created a furor in the house as a servant who witnessed this quickly ran to the Landlord and informed the incident. The landlord along with his assistants rushed to Chandra dragged him out and thrashed him severely.

Deeply dejected with the society, Chandra wrote a letter to his parents and set out to the Himalayas in search of an answer to the calling of his Soul. He was anguished and he felt numbness in his mind.

Selling his watch and using up the little money in his possession, Chandra boarded a train that would take him to Northern India, to the foothills of the Great Himalayas.

The Himalayas or the Snow mountains have been India's boon and a curse. They are the sanctuary to anyone who wanted to lead a recluse life and attain spiritual evolution. They also acted as a natural boundary warding off barbarians from attacking it.

But, the science of geomancy states that it is the Himalayas—as they are situated at Isanya direction or the North East—that makes India a 'Karma Bhoomi' or 'The Land of Karma' In this country, success does not depend purely on hard work and dedication. One has to be free of bad karma and must have the 'luck' to be successful. This is contrary to the United States, where the logical outcome of hard work, passion, dedication and commitment is a definite success.

CHAPTER: TWELVE

Seated below a tree in the front yard of his small ashram, on the banks of river Ganges, engrossed deeply in meditation, Vishwa Dharma resembled a sitting corpse. On either side of him were his disciples who served him. In ancient India, the pupils lived in the Master's house generally called 'Ashram' and they served him and in return he taught them all the subjects. This tradition continues to this day in spiritual pursuits.

Slowly, he opened his eyes and called his disciple.

'Go to the railway station. In one hour, the train from Delhi will make a brief halt. Stand near the last bogie. A person with red color shirt and black color trousers will get down. Tell him that I had sent you and bring him to me?'

'Yes master. What shall I call this person as?'

'His name is Chandra'

Such miracles were not new to his disciples. His Master had the ability to communicate with Gods. He could predict the future. People throng the ashram in the evenings seeking to know answers to their problems. He answers everyone but does not permit anyone to offer him any food or money. He never felt the need to accept any. He is an alchemist and knows the art of turning Copper into Gold.

This art and power to convert Copper and other base metals into Gold has been both a myth and a reality. It has been a myth in the Western countries but a reality in India. Recorded history describes this art as being mastered by people such as Nagarjuna, a Buddhist monk and Vema Reddy or Vemana as he was popularly called.

Countless Hindu monks meditating in the deep crevices of the Himalayan Mountains knew this art. They used it only to purchase basic food and articles for their physical subsistence. It is more of a supernatural power or a Siddhi than an art. Only the accomplished could obtain this power and they never used it for selfish purposes. The Masters could only guide the disciples of certain merits to achieve this power. It was always left to the disciple to practice austerities to gain this knowledge and power.

Sitting in a general class railway compartment, the night before, Chandra had found it hard to sleep. He slept for an hour and in that disturbed sleep, he had a vision of a person with a bald head and saffron robes. 'Get down at Motichur. I am waiting for you' the person said. Chandra had boarded a train from Delhi to reach Rishikesh. He asked his fellow passengers how far Motichur was. It was a station that the train touched almost one hour before reaching Rishikesh

'But, this train does not halt at Motichur'.

Chandra was bewildered to know that there was indeed a station by that name and indeed it was on the Delhi-Rishikesh route.

The vision haunted him again, when he closed his eyes.

'Have faith son. The train will stop at Motichur.'

A few minutes later, the train suddenly came to a screeching halt. The train made an unscheduled stop. Chandra just looked out on the platform. The name of the station 'Motichur' was almost screaming at him.

Without saying a word, he got down. One person in white robes accosted Chandra as he got down on the platform.

'Is your name Chandra?'

'Yes. How do you know my name?'

'Sir, my master Vishwa Dharma had sent me to bring you to the Ashram.'

The person took the bag from Chandra. Like a mesmerized being, Chandra followed him. Moments later, he found himself facing a very bright person in saffron robes. A powerful feeling of devotion overpowered him. Chandra had found his Master. He prostrated before Vishwa Dharma.

'Master, Accept me as your disciple. Show me the path to God realization. My mind is restless. I am a misfit in this society. I seek your refuge.'

CHAPTER: THIRTEEN

That year was 1935. The era was entirely different. The person was also completely different. Born in the family that bears lineage to Boddhi Dharma, the person who is the originator of Zen Buddhism in China and also the one who taught the Chinese how to fight, Vishwa Dharma has been living in Motichur for more than half a century.

His famous ancestor Boddhi Dharma was born in Kanchipuram on borders of Chennai in a South India Brahmin family about 1500 years ago. Later, he converted to Buddhism and migrated to Zhong Guo or China. The word 'Zen' originated from 'Chan' which is the Chinese version of 'Dhyana' or 'Meditation'. The Shaolin temple in China pays Homage to the South Indian monk who had taught them the martial art. Kung Fu and other martial arts originated from the Shaolin temple. It was the Indians who taught the Chinese the martial arts. They had also taught Buddhism. But thousands of years prior to this, the Chinese prayed to the Hindu God of Brahma. Ancient Chinese caves have paintings of Brahma with Chinese features and China was called as 'Cheena Desa.'

Two things ran in the blood. Spirituality and Short temper. As a child, Vishwa was engrossed in spiritual thoughts. Those days, the entire nation was filled with patriotic spirit to drive away the British. In his youth, Vishwa turned into a revolutionary and tried to revive the banned art of 'Kalari Payyettu' which was a traditional martial art of Kerala in India. It was an advanced form of martial art. His forefather had adopted the skills of 'Kalari Payyettu' to evolve the Shaolin martial arts. He was arrested along with his followers and thrown into prison pronounced as dangerous radicals. Strangely, it was in the Prison that Vishwa started looking inside himself rather than outside. It was also a period when he read a lot.

He understood that if he really wanted to realize God, he must arise above all the arguments and sentiments of patriotism, society and self-centered needs. He read about the great personality, Ganapati Vasista Muni who despite his enormous spiritual practice and powers could not see God, as his mind was obsessed about the betterment of his country.

He chose to lead life of a monk. After independence, he visited many temples and ashrams. He found that most of the Gurus were self-centered and were just tantriks who did magic tricks to woo gullible people for the sake of money and fame. He never found any peace of mind.

Finally, he reached his ancestral place of Kancheepuram. There he found the right Guru, the right soul that was sent by God to show path to millions. His name was Chandrasekharendra saraswati or popularly known as Paramacharya of Kanchi Kama Koti peetham.

Paramacharya was a perfect sanyasi or asectic. A sanyasi or a person who had renounced this world always walked to travel from one place to another. He never travelled by trains, cars of planes. He never slept in anyone's houses or hotels. He slept on the floor in the verandah of the host. There was immense power in his personality. He wore 1008 Rudrakshas or holy beads and carried with him the power of Lord Shiva. He was the leader of the Math that was along with 18 others, established and consecrated by the Great Adi Sankara, the one who had cleansed the Hindu religion.

Vishwa Dharma felt electricity pass through every nerve centre of his body. He experienced immense bliss and peace. Saluting the great Guru, he settled in the town taking up a job as a clerk in a company there for his livelihood. He spent rest of the time in deep meditation and reading religious scriptures. Years rolled by. His parents started forcing him to get married. He never showed any interest in married life.

One day, Paramacharya called him and placed his hand on his head. What takes decades of spiritual practice was imbibed in Vishwa in a matter of moments. He had received his enlightenment. Then, the great Guru directed

Vishwa to move to the Himalayan region and lead rest of his life there. Decades of spiritual practice had made Vishwa Dharma reach perfection. He was blessed with all types of Siddhis or Supernatural powers. Now, he has found in Chandra, a disciple who is worthy of his guidance and who has a great mission to accomplish for the humanity.

CHAPTER: FOURTEEN

He slowly removed the glass lid and kept it aside on the table. Placed before him were carefully brushed artifacts—a gold plank and an oval shaped brown color object. The tarnished gold plank had some images and a few letters engraved upon it. These letters appeared badly smudged. Vicky read the words aloud 'Chintamani Rahasya'.

When Vicky touched the brown object, he felt a huge surge of energy flow through him. He felt as though his body and mind had transformed into many times more powerful. He was able to think 100 times more intelligently. He felt as if his brain would explode out of his head. Vicky closed his eyes and went into deep meditation.

'What is happening?' the Professor shouted

Vicky made a gesture with his hand without opening his eyes. He witnessed an extreme white light, almost blinding in its brightness. He went into a state of complete ecstasy. He experienced weightlessness and had a feeling that he could even fly.

He opened his eyes again and placed the object on the table. With shivering hands, he reached for the glass of water kept on the table and finished it in a gulp. 'I want more water', he asked with a roar in his voice. Jenny was stupefied by his actions and she quickly opened a Coke can and placed it before him.

The sugary drink made him better.

'Professor' he exclaimed 'This is no ordinary object. This is the Chintamani stone'

'What is Chintamani?'

'It's a long story. Some of it is shrouded in myth. There are many versions to it. I will tell you what I know. But, this piece of information that is written on this gold plank has much more than is known'

'It's a magic stone. You must have heard about the Philosopher's stone' Vicky remarked.

'Yes. I did'

'Actually', Jenny interfered. 'There is a Peruvian legend attached to it. They believe that about 6 million years ago, a spaceship landed on an island in Titicaca lake and a woman with a long face emerged from it. The Spanish nicknamed her 'Orejones'. She mated with the locals and gave birth to a new race of Andeans. So, even today certain tribes there elongate their faces and make their ears stretched. Coming to our point, she brought a few stones. The Incas called it as Kalla and we call it as the 'Philosopher's stone'.

'Did you say Kalla?' Vicky sounded surprised.

'Yes. Vicky'

'From where I come from the word 'Kallu' in Tamil language means a stone. It's amazing to learn that the Peruvians named the Special stones of Heaven as 'Kalla'. Did you know that the word for 'Catamaran' also emerged from Tamil? It's a combination of two words 'Catta' meaning to tie or tied 'Maram' meaning wood. Catamaran meant pieces of wood tied together. The Mexicans today call a boat as 'Catamaran.'

'And how is Chintamani related to the Philosopher's stone?' intervened Prof. Chris.

'According to Hinduism, there are 3 objects in the Universe that can grant any wish. They are Kalpataru, the magic tree that bestows anything that is asked, Kamadhenu the wondrous cow that grants any boons and the third one is Chintamani, a precious stone that imbibes enormous powers in the man who possesses it. Chintamani stone is believed to have been given by Lord Shiva to a sage called Kapila Muni. Some say that he had returned it to Heavens and yet some maintain that this stone was lost forever.'

'Whoa. Most of what you said now has gone above my head. We need to study this stone more. Whatever is written about it in the past must be co-related. But, lets us have something credible and something that can be backed up by evidence and with scientific approach.' Professor Chris got up from his seat and pointed to the object.

'This object here is so dull and is covered with some kind of bark. How can this be a precious stone Vicky?' asked the Professor.

'Chintamani stone is supposed to energize the person whose Kundalini has awakened. Since mine is awakened . . . .'

'Vicky, I want to see some scientific evidence' Prof. Chris wanted real answers.

'Okay. Here it is then' Vicky took the object and forcibly ripped the thing apart. The outer sheath broke showing a white light green tint stone extremely dazzling.

'Aah' both the professor and Jenny screamed.

'What are you doing? Don't do that! You are destroying it' cried Jenny.

Vicky broke the corky sheath and pieces of it were lying on the table. The stone looked mesmerizing.

'My God, This is indeed a precious stone'. Jenny shouted in excitement. 'But how did you know it was inside this'.

'That's why I am here and I don't deal with nonsense'

'So, can I hold it?' Jenny asked

'Of course'

'Oh. I feel my body shivering' she kept the stone down 'I can't hold it for long. I feel heavy.'

'What is written on the plank?' the Professor asked.

'The word 'Rahasya' means 'Secret' and the gold plank here seem to suggest the secret about Chintamani. But what beats me is why would the ancient Mayans have something like this written in Sanskrit and why would they call it as 'Chintamani'. Where exactly did you find this?'

'Professor Ramos of University of Mexico found it in the deep jungles of Mexico. He discovered a huge temple there. When he and his team went inside the sanctum sanctorum, they found a key stone and when they removed it, a secret passage gave way and they found it in the deep recesses of that way. Someone has kept it as a big secret.' said the professor.

'We need to seriously study the drawings on the plank. They seem to carry a message. It's all depicted in some code form' offered Vicky.

'That is exactly why I called you here. You and Jenny must start working on it' the Professor got up and put on his overcoat. 'Notwithstanding your supernatural theories, I want to know what the heck this stone and the plank are all about.'

'Jenny. I want you to keep this back in the safe locker. We will meet tomorrow and decide how we proceed'. Professor Chris left the room.

CHAPTER: FIFTEEN

Jenny and Vicky spent couple of hours studying the plank. It had many structures of buildings scattered over on it. Some were big in size and some were small. Each building was in a different shape.

'From what I see here Vicky, this is the famous Mayan Temple Chichen Itza. It temple is called Chilambalam.'

'Did you say Chidambaram?'

'Chilambalam. Why?'

'There is s very famous temple of Lord Shiva in Nataraja form in South India. It is called Chidambaram.'

'Oh. Must be a coincidence'

'It is becoming more and more evident that the people from South India had influenced the Mayans thousands of years before Columbus was born. I do not know why no serious research is being conducted in this direction'.

'Oh Vicky, You are so naïve. Do you know how I and Professor Chris are talked about by other anthropologists and historians? They can never accept the fact that the Asians were first settlers of the Americas.'

'Hmm, I can understand. Look here Jenny, this small image here. It has the sign of dancing Shiva. It is the image of Nataraja although very smudged.'

Running down his finger, Vicky saw a familiar structure of Angkor vat of Cambodia.

'I recognize this temple. This is Angkor Vat of Cambodia. This country was called Kamboja in ancient times. This is supposed to be the largest Hindu temple in the world. Now it is in ruins' said Vicky running his finger on the engraving.

'Jenny. Looking at the positioning of these temples, I think the pieces of Chintamani stones are kept at these temples. We need to do more study on each of these places.'

'Most of the sites are in South East Asia and India. Couple of them are in Mexico and Peru'

'We will have to discuss this with Professor Chris tomorrow'.

'I will. I need lot of resources and in-depth knowledge of these places.'

'Let us get a sandwich and I will walk you through the facilities in the campus and walk you to your room'

'I will take you to a nice restaurant to-night Vicky. I will ask my colleague Akila also to join us. She is from Egypt and she is extremely smart.'

'Thanks. Of course, I look forward to it'

By 3:00 in the afternoon, Vicky found himself deeply engrossed in poring through the books in the Library.

There were bits and pieces of information on the Chintamani stone. Unfortunately, all of them were repetitive. He was hungry for more. He tried internet search and then he came across a piece of information that a part of Chintamani stone was at the American Museum of Natural History. He had a word with Jenny about visiting the museum.

'It's too late Vicky. We can go there first thing tomorrow morning'.

It is common knowledge that Chintamani is a very precious stone. But, it is known to have been broken down to many pieces. A few learned men believed that there were only 3 pieces. One went to the rulers of the east right from Chegiz Khan, who seems to have earned his ferocity due to the power of this stone, which was then passed on it his grand grandson Akbar of India. After that there was no news about the whereabouts of that particular stone.

The second piece was brought by the Russian artist Nicholas Roerich who had presented it to the League of Nations and took it back when that international organization collapsed. He claimed to take it back to the mythical 'Shambala' and returned it to the 'Ruler of the World' to be finally untied with the Mother Stone. Many people call it a big hoax. No one believed that a person could go to Heaven and talk to Gods, much less this Russian painter. But, surprisingly no one pursued his claims seriously. Some suggested that he left it at a Tibetan monastery.

The third and the actual Mother Stone of Chintamani is supposed to be somewhere in the Hindu Kush Mountains or somewhere in the Himalayas. No one knew exactly where it was.

It is surprising that the fourth piece has emerged in the American Museum of Natural History.

And now he has the fifth piece found in a Mayan temple. Could it be that other pieces are buried in all the temple sites depicted on the plank? Why was the stone broken into pieces? Why were the pieces scattered across the

Globe? Who spread them at such long distances? What was the reason? What was the reason for the secrecy behind this stone? Are the Holy Grail stories indeed related to Chintamani?

These questions gave an itch in his mind. His journey had just begun. Not in his wildest dreams did Vicky think how eventful this journey would be. For this was no ordinary stone and there was much more to this than that was written in the books.

But, for now, he needed some rest before getting ready for the dinner with Jenny and Akila. He realized that he did not bring anything from India as compliments for anyone. Then he remembered that his mother had sent 2 sets of Ganapati idols. Ganapati or Ganesh or Vignesh or Vinayaka is the God of obstacles. Hindus believed that praying to this God who has the divine body with head of an Elephant, can make the obstacles and hurdles vanish. He was the first God to whom respects are offered. He set the 2 small boxes aside for the girls.

CHAPTER: SIXTEEN

They agreed to meet at 7:00 and so they did. Jenny was there with Akila Hassan and the introductions were brief and business-like. Jenny planned to take them to Zorba's brother, a nice small Greek Diner that served sumptuous food.

'The place where we are going is right across the street' she said.

'Should we take the truck Jenny? Can't we walk?' asked Akila.

'No. Not after you had eaten at that place. You will be so full that you would be able to barely walk' she chuckled.

They hopped in and after a few minutes, Vicky found himself gaping at the Menu not knowing what to order for the entrée . . . He loved Greek salad and it was easy to find and also the double chocolate cake. Finally, he settled for Lemon Garlic Chicken. It sounded closer to home. The girls had ordered platters and some special entrée.

'So, I heard that you guys had trouble with the relic and it seemed to be sending a strange electro-magnetic interruption. Is it some kind of a special stone that have discovered like the Philosopher's stone today.' Akila remarked.

'Yeah, Sort of . . . It is called the Chintamani stone'. Vicky corrected.

'There are many powerful objects nature had given to the Mankind. I am a Muslim and some of us believe that our Rasool Allah had placed special divine stones in the Kaaba. These stones were White in color with green tint when he placed them originally and it seems due to its absorbing all the bad energies from the human beings making them pure and good-hearted.' Akila said.

'That is something wonderful Akila. There are so many dimensions to this subject that I honestly do not know where to start'. Vicky stretched back.' There is a debate going on amongst scholars if and whether the Chintamani stone, the Philosopher's stone and the Holy Grail are the same or different. We know how the Knights Templar protected it with zeal and also the hapless Cathars."

'We also need scientific evidence to back our claims. I think Noetic science has evolved to provide empirical evidence in such matters' suggested Akila.

'Yes. There is a common purpose in all of them. They have the capacity to elevate Man into divine being with Supernatural powers. The possessor also gains the knowledge of converting any base metal into Gold. Once he gets this knowledge, he can use the power of this stone and his own power to do so.'

Jenny interfered, 'Vicky. I have forgotten to mention this. Professor Chris called me. He said that he will have to call for a Press Conference. This is a major discovery and the entire world will be interested to know.'

'When does he plan to do that?'

'In couple of days, he said that we should all come up with a preliminary note on this by tomorrow evening.'

'Jenny. Tomorrow morning I want to visit the American Museum of Natural History. They have a piece of Chintamani stone. We must start early I guess.'

'No problem, we can visit it tomorrow'

'So Vicky, I heard about your new area of study of Occult in Ancient India. Well. I have been studying Ancient Egypt and I want to share something which you might already know' Akila wanted to learn something useful for her research.

She began. 'The ancient Egyptians believed that the first settlers had come from the land of Punt and this Punt is believed to be Kerala. Are you sure?'

'May be Kerala, But you must also bear in mind that there were many islands in Western India those days. Going by the geographical description, I think it is either Kerala or lands adjacent to it. From what I had learnt, an ancient Indian king by name 'Puru' was the source of the word 'Pharaoh'. His Grandson's name was Manasyu. He was actually Menes, who the historians claim to be the first Egyptian king. The name 'Egypt' itself originated from 'Ajapati', who was an ancient king of the Sun dynasty, who prayed to the Sun or 'Ravi', hence the Egyptian Sun God, 'Ra'.'.

Jenny interrupted 'So, you guys are saying that the Egyptians are from India. Don't they look very different than Indians?'

Vicky explained. 'No civilization worth its salt would attribute their origins to another civilization, if it were not the truth. Moreover, in India we have people of various gene pools. Some of them had migrated from Africa. Ancient India had links with Zanzibar. It was known as Shankh Dvip—the island of shells. The word 'Shankh' later was mispronounced as 'Zanzi'. Most people still theorize that Mount Meru of Tanzania is the same mountain that was written in Hindu texts. Somalia was supposed to be the kingdom of Sumali, uncle of Demon Ravan.'

Just then the food was served on the table and Vicky stopped speaking.

'Please continue'

'It is fashionable to believe that the first humans emerged from Ethiopia. But, long before that, cowrie shells from Indian Lakshadweep were found in Ethiopia. Africans used cowrie shells as currency. The problem lies with the attitude of a few Western Scholars. They do not give any cognizance to the discovery of the submerged city of Dwarka off the coast of Gujarat in India, which proves that Indian epics are not just fiction but a reality. They are obsessed with Greek civilization and assume that everything that is good and great originated in Greece.'

'Is it not true that there are many similarities between Indian and Greek civilizations?' asked Akila.

'Yes. There are. The ancient Greeks burnt the dead bodies on funeral pyre just like the Hindus. Their priests wore white cloths as we did and some of them shaved their heads as we did. The ancient Indians and Greeks traded a lot. Indian fabrics, precious stones, spices and colors were the favorite in ancient Greece. Their classics Iliad and Homer bear close resemblance to the Hindu epics of Ramayana and Mahabharata. Most of the characters have similarities in Hindu mythology. In fact Panini in his Sanskrit Grammar had written about them. The Greeks were called 'Yavanas'. Both the civilizations knew the art of riding horses and chariots'.

He ate a little salad and continued.

'I read somewhere that when Alexander went to invade India, almost 10,000 of his soldiers were devotees of Krishna, Is it not strange that although in those days when we had many historians in India, no one gave much significance to Alexander's adventure. It was just considered to be a simple skirmish on the Indian borders. But, the Greek historians went panicky explaining the reasons for Alexander returning back.'

'There are strong connections with Egypt too. I read that Mummies were unearthed in Harappa and Mohenjodaro that looked similar to the Egyptian Mummies. Did you know that the Muslin cloth that was used to wrap the Mummies came from India? India supplied some of the ingredients used in the process of mummification.' Akila tried to bring the Egyptian perspective.

'I heard about it Akila. But, apart from that I have been trying to establish more connections between these two grand civilizations. I will need lot of your help.'

'Sure Vicky.'

Vicky continued 'Here is something that will excite you. John Hanning Speke was a British explorer who wanted to find out the source of River Nile. The local Egyptians could not help him. After lot of research, he we visited India to seek help of the Brahmins in Varanasi city and it was there when they had guided him to Lake Victoria. In ancient scriptures the river was named as Nila Amara. 'Nila' became 'Nile' and 'Amara' was astonishingly the area on the north east corner of Victoria N'yanza. How could the Hindus know so accurately about the geography of Africa? This is a big mystery.'

'Incredible. You seem to have done lot of research' Akila complemented.

'It is my job.'

'And which is why I invited her over. We have lot of work to do in the days to come.' Jenny broke her silence.

'Yes. We do. We will come out with a Press release by tomorrow evening. The food is excellent here Jenny. Thank you very much for the wonderful meal and even more wonderful company'.

CHAPTER: SEVENTEEN

He had given each of the girls, the idols of Ganapati. They were so pleased with the gifts.

'Is it not a big co-incidence that I am gifting you these idols of Ganapati, who is believed to have brought back the stolen Chintamani stone to Sage Kapila? The sage then sought the presence of Ganapati instead of Chintamani. There is a temple in South India by name Chintamani Ganapati.'

'You know Akila. Vicky is very religious. You should have seen him this morning when he touched the Stone. He went into raptures'. Jenny giggled. 'But, jokes apart that stone has tremendous positive energy. I could feel it'

'I can't wait to see it. I hope the Professor would not mind.' asked Akila.

'The Professor is taking it lightly. He will only believe when we give him empirical evidence about the stone. Moreover, Professor Ramos who had brought this stone and the plank from Mexico is yet to recover from the fever. We expect him to be alright by tomorrow.'

'So, would this mean that the Stone goes back to Mexico?' Vicky wanted to know how much time he has to complete his job.

'I do not know the protocol Vicky. But, looks like that the moment we give enough evidence about the stone being Chintamani or a part of Chintamani, then it will be under high security surveillance. Whether Mexican Government will be willing to let it remain in the United States or whether it will ask for it is left to them.'

'We are taking this very easily Jenny. If the same thing were to happen back in India, it would have created Media frenzy by now. We have more than 250 news channels of all sorts that would love to make this as their headlines' said Vicky.'

After the dinner, they went back to the truck.

Vicky ran back into the restaurant and asked for the washroom. He ran into it and threw up horribly all the food he had eaten. Worried, Jenny and Akila ran after him. They waited for him outside the washroom.

'It's all right. I am okay now. I think it's the food'.

The Captain of the restaurant was concerned. He offered Vicky to sit and brought him some Lemonade. 'On the house, sir'

He drank the Lemonade. 'Are you okay Vicky? Or do you need to see a doctor?' asked Akila.

'I am okay. I am a bit shaken now. When I was throwing up, I had visions of bright light and some noises. I should not have eaten any meat today, as I had touched the Chintamani.'

'You are very gullible and superstitious. We had discussed that Chegiz Khan had part of this stone. Don't you know that he was such a horrible guy and he used to drink the blood of his enemies after killing them?' Jenny said. 'When nothing bad happened to him, nothing bad should happen to you. You need to settle down a little. It's just a change of food and water'

'Jenny, you are nice. Thanks for your concern. I think I am okay now. Let's go'

The girls gave him a partial hug saying 'Good night' after dropping him at the quarters. As he walked into his room, Vicky felt delusional. He started having bouts of bright visions. He just fell on the bed and started praying. He will need lot of praying in the coming days. The events that were set in motion will take toll on him.

He woke up middle of the night. He removed his shoes and sent a mail to Prof. Sastry. He had put all the questions in his mind about the Chintamani stone. Although Vicky was supposed to be an expert in this subject, he wanted the perspective of Subbu Sastry. The research community thought Subbu Sastry was a nut case as he had held some mind blowing explanations and theories on every subject. Vicky needed to know all those theories. He had to get the facts. He marked the subject 'Urgent.'

CHAPTER: EIGHTEEN

Going for a walk around the campus on a wintry morning was not a right thing to do. But, he had heard about the Greatness of Rixton University and morning is a good time to see the buildings.

Before setting out for the day, Vicky had checked his email. His uncle wanted to know his whereabouts and ended the mail with the usual 'call me' note. Prof. Sastry replied his mail with a bizarre explanation.

'Vicky, I am happy to learn about your work. Chintamani is no ordinary stone. It is the stone that had given the Demon Ravan his power. If you have read the Ramayana, you would have guessed it already. The life force and the great powers of Ravan were stored in his abdomen in form of this hard stone. As long as this was part of Ravan's body, he could not be killed. That is why, when the Wind God directed the arrow towards his abdomen, it broke the

Chintamani into many pieces and Ravan died. No matter how many bad things that evil Ravan had done in his life, he was after all, one of the greatest devotees of Shiva and his prayers had empowered and supported him. Do you know that it took around 1,000 years for Ravan's body to be burnt? Later, the stone and the pieces were taken by his brother Vibheeshan and they got dispersed around the world over a period of time.

The story of Shiva granting this stone to Sage Kapila is also true. But, remember that Kapila Sage returned it to Shiva and so, it was given to Ravan.

Now, that is broken into many pieces, its power would have reduced a lot. Vicky, it is amazing that this stone was found in Mexico. It is believed that one of the Mayan kings had this stone on his crown.

And what is this nonsense you talk about that Russian guy Roerich? He never had any Chintamani stone. If his stone was a genuine Chintamani, then why did the League of Nations fail when he had gifted it to them? And why did he take it back when the League collapsed? That was just a publicity stunt. Did you see his paintings? He had painted the Chintamani stone as placed on a Bull and the so called Ruler of the World was Lord Shiva. Shambala land which Roerich claims to be the land of Gods is Kailash. If he had promised to give the stone back to Shambala in Tibet, what is the piece doing in that Museum in New York? He also claimed to have given another piece to

Moscow Museum. He had made a fool of this world and it included you and Jennifer.

Vicky felt dazed after reading the Professor's explanation. He was aware of many of personal shortcomings of his own although he had always believed that he was destined to do something remarkable in life. He had developed a restless mind since childhood. He felt out of pace in normal social situations. His tolerance threshold was extremely limited. Over the years, his heightened sense of consciousness sensitized him further. He was a liberal and yet gets extremely restless if anything imperfect was around him. He had an antenna to read the human thoughts. He easily felt the strength of negative vibrations from other minds.

He detested most of the new songs. If the lyrics of the movie songs were awful, the music was terrible. Art, he always maintained must reform the society or in the least enlighten it, not to corrupt it and not to debase the cultural standards. Although, there was bad music and extremely bad lyrics in the American music, the music that was generally played on the Radio and the public places was of good quality.

He had developed special allergy to a few particular music composers who shamelessly plagiarized their music from Central Asian countries of Khuzestan, Turkmenistan, Tajikistan, Uzbekistan and Kyrgyzstan. They scramble the music and made a mish mash of it changing the notes from Minor to Major and vice versa and changed the equation of the pace, giving it a distinct touch of originality. Except for a few music lovers with exposure to international music, no one realized this duplicity. Honestly, no one bothered to even care. He sometimes wondered how people could tolerate such absolute trash.

In comparison, India had great music talent in the past. The songs had a balance of vocals and music. When vocals dominated, the music took the back seat and vice versa. Music must elevate a person to higher planes of thought and it must purely entertain. The modern day music was not 'Entertainment'. It was 'Exitainment' The music of regional languages in India was much worse than Hindi which fared a lot better comparatively. To neutralize this he always plugged in ear phones that played a medley of Zen music, Western Classical music and his favorite Carnatic music

Vicky keyed in a sober reply. 'Professor, please share with me any proof to substantiate your theory? Did you actually verify the authenticity of the stone in the Museum?'

He was very eager to learn more about Chintamani. Jenny picked him up and they started the day at work with a cup of Brazilian Coffee, which had its unique flavor. Vicky had stopped pining for his South Indian Filter Coffee in the morning.

CHAPTER: NINETEEN

'Can we go to the American Museum of Natural History now Jenny?' Vicky was extremely curious to compare the Chintamani stone there with the one which he had seen the day before.

'Vicky. Yes. But, I have some paper work to do. I have to talk to the Public Relations and make arrangements for the Press Conference. It will take half-an-hour at the most. I have to call the guys at the lab and ask them to test this stone today. In the mean time, you can wait here'

As Jenny set on to work, Vicky was lost in his thoughts. There are many unanswered questions. If Roerich had pieces of Chintamani stone and if it was indeed so powerful, what made the League of Nations fail indeed as Professor Sastry remarked? Was he having the Chintamani or did he get confused with some other stone? The piece in the Museum will answer this.

It is strange that he did not get much time to talk to Jenny about Roerich. She must have some knowledge on this. Or rather I should meet the Professor Chris and find out what he knows about Roerich's involvement with the Chintamani stone.

'Jenny. Is the Professor in?'

'Yes. He is.'

'Can I see him?'

'Sure. Let me call him' She called him and the Professor was talking to Professor Ramos in his room. He asked Vicky to come in.

Being the head of the department and a senior professor, Chris enjoyed certain privileges. If it were some other time, Vicky would have taken interest in all the photographs, shields, medals and other stuff in the Professor's office. Right now, his mind was entangled with questions that overwhelmed him.

'Good morning professor. How are you doing today?'

'I am doing good. Vicky. I want you to meet Professor Ramos from Mexico. He is the one who had discovered the stone and the gold plank'

'How do you do, I am Vikram Reddy. You can call me Vicky. I heard about the accident. How are you feeling now Professor?'

'I am fine now Vicky. Thank you for your concern. I am truly excited about the discovery. We found this near an excavation. The place itself seemed to have missed the onslaught of Bishop Diego Da Landa and Hernando Cortez. Fortunately, the temple priests had hidden these objects in a secret passage'

'Can you give more details Professor?' asked Vicky.

'Let me explain briefly. It's a tragic story of complete annihilation of a culture and race that occurred between 1519 and 1533. The over enthusiastic preachers from Europe were extremely cruel and narrow minded. Bishop Diego Da Landa wanted to preach Christianity and so he and his fanatics destroyed all the temples, demolished the idols and statues burnt all the Holy Scriptures and branded the people as demon-worshippers and either converted them or killed them. Hernando Cortez was worse. He slaughtered in millions and in one instance when people had hidden in a temple patio, he massacred six thousand people including women and children in a matter of two hours.'

'My God' cried Vicky.

'Yes. But there are incredible similarities between the America's first civilizations and India. You must be aware that the Peruvian Aztecs believed themselves to be descendants of the Sun dynasty in which your epic hero, Ram was part of. That is why even to this day, the largest festival celebrated by them goes by the name 'Ram-Sitva' meaning Ram Sita'

'Amazing, I and Jenny were discussing it'

'There is a lot more. The Mayans followed the Geomancy principles of South India. Their architecture was based on the person Asura Maya who was the chief builder for the Asuras of Patal loka which was what the Hindus called the American continent as. They followed the concept of 8 blocks of 8 feet each, making 64 square feet as a unit of Vastu Purusha'

'Professor, I admire your in-depth knowledge on this subject. There are many similarities between the Mayans with the Hindu civilization.'

'I have been focusing my study on the religious connection as well Vicky. Your Virabhadra is our Viracocha. Your Kubera is our Tezcatlipoca. Your Narasimha is our Narsingha. Your Indra is our Xiuhtechutli and your Agni is our Xipe Totec. If you observe the temple architecture, both the Indian and Mayan temples had their upper most area of the tower exactly one-fourth of the bottom. The ancient Mayans believed in the concept of 'Kuntalini' which is 'Kundalini' in India. The Mayans also believed in the concept of

'Chaklas' which are 'Chakras' and they spelt 'Yoga' as 'Yoka".

'Sir, I think the ancient Mayan civilization had indeed migrated from South India. Do you agree?' asked Vicky.

'Either that or it would have been influenced by the conquerors and seafarers from South India. The Mexicans call the boat as 'Catamaran' which is a South Indian word. But the Kekichi tribe of Mayans of Guatemala, who flourished 2,000 years ago, maintained that their ancestors had travelled from Nagaland and the DNA tests confirmed the genetic connection between the Naga tribes and the Mexican tribes. You will find this amusing. But, my name Ramos and Ramirez is supposed to be derived from your Hindu epic hero. Ram.'

'It must have been a perilous journey those days. Most of the migrations must have taken place from South India by sea.'

'It happened both ways. The Nagas had migrated through Siberia. The Bering straits area those days had icy sheet connecting both the landmasses. They walked down the Canadian and American territory until they found the warmer climate of Mexico and Latin America. The South India and South East Asia were partners in trade and cultural exchange with the Americas. We have a term called 'Asio American civilizations' to describe our ancient civilizations.

Most of the evidence had been destroyed by these and religious fanatics from Europe. They never wanted the truth to come out. Moreover, your own Indian Government after independence did not care to show attention to the legacy of ancient Hindus. I do not understand why?'

'It is sad and bad politics Professor. Our first Prime Minister Pt. Jawaharlal Nehru was an atheist. Although, he had written two voluminous books on Indian and the World History, he did not care to establish the roots with other countries. He did not want the Hindus to be seen as a great community. He was confident of their vote bank. He had to woo the minorities in India. His mentor Gandhi was one step worse. He always feared that Hindus would dominate the country and therefore wanted the minorities to rule the country. The British cared less. Moreover, once Godse, a Hindu fanatic killed Gandhi, no one thought it was safe to speak in favor of Hinduism'

'It is strange Vicky. I had been to South East Asia and was amazed to see how Hindu concepts still guide their way of life. It's a subject for another day. But today, I am glad to show you the similarities. There is lot of similarity in food habits. South Indians eat lot of spicy food. So do the Mexicans. Your Roti is similar to our Tortillas. The Quechua language is similar to your Sanskrit. Our Pattoli game is the similar to your Pachisi game. There are so many other similarities. You must visit Mexico, Peru, Guatemala and other surrounding countries and you will discover more.'

'Sir, I am curious to know as you why the Mayans falsely believe that the world would come to an end in the year 2012.'

'There was no mention of the end of the world Vicky. It surely had noted the end of the Calendar and an era. The next continuing calendar went missing and it was later found in another cave. Although it is true that some doomsayers say that as the Mayan Calendar ended there, human civilization also ended with it. Do you know that the Mayan Calendar had lot of similarities with the Hindu calendar? There were only a few years of difference between the starting of Cycles. The Mayan Calendar began around 3112 B.C., and the Hindus believed that the Iron Age or Kali Yuga started in the year 3102 B.C. That is because the Mayans had followed the Venus calendar. The last day of this phase of history was earmarked to be December 21, 2012, in this grand cycle of evolution. The Mayans used calendrics system to quantify vast periods of time and I learnt that South Indians are the only other people who use calendrics in time measurement. Perhaps, the Mayans learnt it from the Indians.'

Vicky replied. 'Yes. It originated from the area where I hail from Tamilnadu. The ancient Tamilians used a calendar that used calendrics. Even today, they refer to it. It is called 'Tirukkanda Panchanga' or 'The Secret doctrine'.

'The reason why the Mayan Calendar ended was the difference between Hindu and the Mayan Calendars was that the Hindu Calendar was based on Jupiter as the Suras or Gods believed Jupiter to be their teacher and the Mayans adopted Venus as the reference for their Calendar as the Asuras believed Sukra to be their teacher' explained Prof. Ramos.

Jenny entered the room and briefed the Professor. Vicky shook hands with Professor Ramos. 'Sir, I truly appreciate your tremendous knowledge. I am eager to see you again'.

'I am eager to see you too Vicky. You seem to be cracking the puzzle of the stone.'

'I am doing my best sir'.

Then Vicky turned to Professor Chris.

'Professor, I wanted to know more about Nicolas Roerich as he is closely connected to the Chintamani stone'

'I heard about Nicholas Roerich but I did not care to learn anything about him because I really do not believe in Occult and super natural concepts. I can't help you there. But, you can talk to one William Pierce who is an expert on this subject. In fact, he is expected here this afternoon.'

'Yes sir. I will meet him' Vicky greeted Professor Chris and shook hands with Prof. Ramos before leaving the room along with Jenny.

CHAPTER: TWENTY

The traffic near the George Washington Bridge was insane. Jenny was extra-ordinarily calm that morning. She had seen many rough days in her life. Her mother was a drug addict and it was a miracle that Jenny survived the delivery. Her mother died due to complications. Her aunt had taken care of little Jennifer. Her aunt Mary was a school teacher and did not have any kids. Jennifer came into her life as a bundle of joy. Mary's husband John Green was a counter salesman at the local grocery store. Although he was a nice person, he had drinking problem.

The early years of Jenny's life went without much of an event. But, when she turned twelve, her problems began. John started drinking heavily and often fought with Mary. On her part Mary tried her best to keep things quiet at home. John had a big inferior complex. Whenever there was anything remotely associated with Mary's family, he went ballistic with his false accusations on her. Mary hailed from a very rich family. She loved John, but her parents did not approve of him. She left the house and married John and they lived in an old single bedroom house.

It was difficult for Mary to maintain the household with her paltry income and John's income. But, she always took care of Jennifer. When Jenny turned Fourteen, one day John did not return home. She and Mary waited outside the house for his return. They did not even have a phone at home. At about 10'O clock a Police car drove to their house. Two officers, one who was a lady, approached them and said something to Mary. Mary started weeping aloud. The lady cop tried to console her. Jenny knew something terrible had happened. It did not take much time for her to know that John had died in a road accident. He was awfully drunk and crossed the street and was hit by a truck. He was taken to the hospital where he died.

Jenny found it very difficult to keep up with the world. Her friends at school went out on weekends. She did not. They went on vacations. She stayed at home. At that age, she was way too innocent to understand the cruelty of the world. After a few months, Mary talked to her. Jenny had to find some errand job if they had to survive.

They moved to a smaller place on a shabby corner. Mary was able to save couple of hundred dollars by doing so. After school, she moonlighted, acting as a waitress at a local restaurant. Jenny found it difficult to find a job due to her age. She finally got a job at a meat packing company as a worker. The owner of the company was a Mexican and he did not care what the law said. He hired Jenny and she had to slog her evening hours, weighing the meat and packing it in polythene bags and seal them. She worked between six in the evening until ten in the night. Things went normal for couple of years.

Jenny juggled with her studies, work and chores at home. She never had a chance for entertainment or the inclination for it. Life went on mechanically. One day, the owner of the meat packing unit died. The following week, his Son took over the company. Young Jenny at 16 did not know the ways of the world. She was way too innocent.

One evening when she went to work, she found no one. Her new boss, Jose Soto was sitting in his small glass cabin in the corner. She went inside and asked if there was no work for the day. Jose walked out of the cabin and pulled down the shutter. Jenny was molested that night. She cried and she protested. She was helpless. Jose threatened her with a knife. He threatened her that if she revealed this to anyone, he would kill her and Mary. Jenny did not utter a word.

Her dress was torn. Outside it was cold. She did not bother to even wear her jacket. Her mind had gone numb. Jenny was poor. She was weak. But, she was not dumb and she was not a coward. She walked up to the main road and walked until she found a police officer. She reported what had happened.

Jose was arrested. Jose's lawyer tried to taint Jenny's character. But, nothing worked. Jose was sentenced and as a penalty, he was made to pay Jenny a sum of half a million dollars. Jose had to sell his business, his house. She and Mary moved to a better city in New Jersey. Mary opened a bakery there and it was an instant success. Life started being good. Jenny stopped working. She assisted Mary whenever she had free time.

She now worked hard and obtained scholarship for college education. She never let her fate take her spirits away. She fought and made her own destiny. After college, she continued her research at the Rixton University.

Many guys proposed to her. She never found anyone interesting. She wanted someone really brilliant and really good at heart. With her growing age, her nerves got harder. She easily lost her temper. She became very impatient. But that particular day she was very calm. She for a moment wondered if that was the effect of the stone she had touched the day before.

They reached the museum. Vicky was awed by its sheer size and the collection of this great museum. Had it been another day, he would have spent the entire day looking at the artifacts and the history gallery. Now, he wanted to head straight to the case where the Chintamani stone was kept.

CHAPTER: TWENTY ONE

Jenny was accompanied by the Museum supervisor. It was important that they inspect the stone thoroughly. They closed that particular section for ten minutes.

'Ten minutes is all that I can give you' the supervisor said placing the stone before Vicky. The stone looked ordinary. Although, there was a Green tint to it, it looked more like a Green crystal. Vicky held it in his hand to feel the energy. He felt nothing at all. He inspected it closely to see any signs. There were none. Jenny inspected the stone. She photographed the stone with her digital camera. They did not require ten minutes. Their job was done in five minutes.

'Sir, Is there any other place where Roerich could have placed pieces of this stone?'Vicky asked.

'It is a mystery. Some say he gave it to the United Nations. Some say that he laid it as the foundation stone for the

Master Building in Manhattan and some say that he took it back to Tibet.

On their drive back, Vicky engaged into a conversation unrelated to their pursuit. 'So, Jenny tell me. Do you think the world will end soon, even though the Mayans had got the date wrong?'

'Vicky, there are many theories going around. This is the one closer home. What may happen is that the Earth would shift its poles that day. It is indeed possible that this could happen in a matter of days or hours. Albert Einstein confirmed its possibility. Our own scientists at the Rixton University confirmed that 800 Million Years ago, the Equator had passed through Alaska and what is Equator now was Polar region. This shift will mean global catastrophe and will wipe out majority of life as we know it on this planet.

'Are you aware of Merlin?' Jenny asked breaking her lecture.

'Oh you mean the Magician Merlin of King Arthur times?'

'No. There is an older guy named Merlin in the 5th Century. He had prophesied many events of the future. His prophecies became popular in the 11th Century. He had predicted global disaster in the first half of the 21st century and said that the planets would shift their orbits. It could only happen when there is a Polar shift on Earth.'

'It is really scary Jenny. But, something tells me we will survive'

'The Oracle of Delphi also had predicted this event. There was a Native American Prophet called Black Elk. He too predicted that half the people on the Earth would die. The Hoppi tribes who are Native Americans also believe that the world would come to an end. They cited the events that were occurring now before that. They had in fact written that this will come about by a device called Spider web. This should relate to the Web-bot project'.

'Wow Jenny. You know so much on this subject'

Vicky was very impressed with Jenny. She was sincere and hard working.

'I am truly impressed. But, tell me this. What is this Web-bot project' asked Vicky.

'Web-bot project was started in the 1990s to predict the stock market movements. But, over the years, it developed into such a massive enterprise, that it captured the collective conscious of all the web users around the globe. It predicted the 9/11 attack, the Tsunami and also Hurricane Katrina. The project says a major catastrophe will occur in the first half of 21st century. Remember. It's the computer speaking.'

She continued 'I am aware of planet Nibiru. In fact it belongs to the neighboring dark star. It cuts through our Solar system once in every 3,600 years. One of these revolutions caused the destruction of one of the planets in our solar system. There was a big planet between Mars and Jupiter. If you see the orbits of our solar system, you will find a large gap between Mars and Jupiter. But that particular orbit is filled with Asteroids and dwarf planets. In fact millions of years ago, there was a big planet there. It is believed that one of the Moons of Nibiru planet hit it and destroyed it completely, smashing it into small pieces. Now, many scientists believe that this hot planet Nibiru or one of its moons will hit the Earth sometime during this generation. NASA is aware of it. There is a conspiracy theory that the Government is aware of the danger, but has chosen not to reveal to the public.'

'Well. NASA does a great job and its Deep Space Projects keeps a watchful eye in the Space.'

'Yes it is Vicky. But, tell me. What is it that you and I can do if something like that were to happen?' Jenny smiled.

'My intuition says that nothing of that sort will ever happen. If it does we have enough technology available. I read somewhere that NASA has now developed ion drive rockets that can change the direction of these objects and if there are surprises, I can just pray.'

There were moments of intense silence. Then Vicky opened his bag and made a few notes. He went through the digital images Jenny had taken of the stone in the Museum. They were back in the University by late afternoon.

CHAPTER: TWENTY TWO

William Pierce and Akila were studying the stone when Vicky and Jenny entered the Study. Akila introduced Vicky to William.

Although William Pierce did not have much of academic qualification to warrant an expert dialog, he was the only source of expertise on the subject of Nicholas Roerich and supposedly the legend of Chintamani stone.

'So, where exactly to you hail from in India?' William asked.

'Chennai'

'Chennai. I know that city. It is the head quarters of Theosophical society. Roerich, Madam Blavatsky, Annie Besant, President Roosevelt and many other eminent people from the United States were its members. It is a

hidden truth that Gandhi and Nehru were also members'
William started.

'That is correct sir. Now, I am very curious to know about
Nicholas Roerich from you.'

William moved toward a table and pulled a chair and sat.
Vicky sat in front of him.

'Nicholas Roerich was a Russian mystic and a painter.
He had made many paintings. He and his wife Helena
Roerich visited France in the year 1923. While they stayed
in a luxury apartment, they claim that they had received a
Pinewood box with the sender's name written as 'Banker's
Trust'. In that box, there was a Rajput casket. When they
opened the casket, they found the Chintamani stone. He
found a few letters in Sanskrit engraved on the stone. He
translated it into a message. 'Through the Stars I come. I
bring the chalice covered with the shield.'

'Incredible'

'The Secret societies believed that Humans originated
from Sirius star system and anything related to the Sirius
star was sacred. Nicholas Roerich had many powerful
followers. One of them was the then Secretary of
Agriculture of the U.S.Government, Henry Wallace in the
FDR administration. In fact President Roosevelt himself
was influenced by Roerich . . . In one of the letters Wallace
had shown enthusiasm that Roerich would bring the
Foundation stone of the New world to the United States.

For a layman these words appear harmless. But to the one who knows about the secret societies, it is obvious that the New world or the One World concept was the core theme of Illuminati and Theosophists. In fact Helena Roerich had stated that she is often visited by the spirit of one Master Moraya. The same Master Moraya was believed to have inspired Madam Blavatsky in being a Gnostic. Gnostic is a person who believed in Satan.'

'What? Do you mean to say that Madam Blavatsky was a Satan Worshipper? I have not heard anything remotely as this about the Theosophical society' protested Vicky.

'Did you observe their symbol?' asked William.

'Yes. They had a sign of Aum and a Cross in it'

'What about the snake that ate its own tail? That is the symbol of Satan' explained William.

'Not only Blavatsky, but all those who followed her philosophy. She wrote in her book 'The Secret Doctrine' the base line 'Demon est dues inversus' meaning 'Devil is God inverted'. She believed that in the Eden Garden the serpent that tempted Eve was the Angel of Light and the God who prohibited Man from partaking in the Tree of Knowledge was indeed Evil. 'Gnosis' means 'to know' So, this philosophy ran contrary to the traditional ecclesiastical belief system.'

'Its your interpretation sir. In the East the snake is not considered to be evil' Vicky defended Theosophical Society.

'Coming back to our story, Roerich took the box to Darjeeling India around 1928—29 and according to his assistant, Sin Fozdick; he placed the image of Maitreya.'

'Do you mean Maitreya, the pending incarnation of Buddha?'

'Yes. People such as Roerich and Madam Blavatsky believed in his arrival to redeem the world and to punish the Sinners'

'In Hinduism we expect Kalki Bhagwan to do that.'

'Quite right, But, these people were too rigid to accept Hinduism. Buddhism gave them lot of space to be flexible. So, along with the image of Maitreya, he placed an image of Master Moraya and a personal letter signed by Roerich himself along with a few coins and the Chintamani Stone. Then this box was shipped to Manhattan New York and this was placed in the Cornerstone of Master Building which was constructed and funded by one of Roerich's wealthy disciple Louis Horch'

Vicky was eager to visit this building. 'Wow. I heard about this at the Museum. What is the specialty of this building?'

William continued. 'The Master Building is huge one. It was built exclusively to host Roerich's paintings and for his artistic and spiritual pursuits. It is on 103rd on Riverside Drive. You can still see the corner stone in marble where the casket was buried. When the building's corner stone was laid down, many Governments had sent their diplomats. People such as Einstein and Tagore sent letters.'

'If it was so important, why did Roerich himself not carry it to the United States?'

'Good question. Roerich had played well with the public and the he somehow managed to make Wallace believe that the real Chintamani stone was with him. After a few days, Wallace being the Agriculture secretary, commissioned Roerich to visit Asia to do research on drought and dry regions in Asia with an aim to grow vegetation in desert. But, Roerich used this position to invite regional chiefs n Tibet and started working towards a One Asia.'

'The concept of One World Government?'

'Yes. It was a step in the direction towards that Utopia. Due to this, he was suspected as of being an Asian spy and this diluted his goodwill with Wallace and FDR. He also lost the patronage of Louis Horch, And then the paintings were moved to a small building which is now called the 'Roerich Museum"

'Sir, why are there so many versions to the Roerich's stones?'

'Unfortunately, no one knows the truth. Helena called these stones Terephims. Terephims, according to Judaism and the Old Testament stones and idols believed to give a person all comforts and good things in life. Rachel, daughter of Laban stole if from her father and eloped with Jacob and as she feared that the stones would be traced, she hid them in her skirts'

'I remember some parts of this story' Vicky recollected.

'Do you know that according to the New Testament and according to the secret scrolls buried deep in the Vatican cellars, Magi Balthasar had given this stone as the fourth gift to the Holy Child? It is rumored that Pope Gregory had commissioned a team to search for this stone'

'No. I am not aware. It looks like this stone has quiet a remarkable place in all the religions' observed Vicky.

'Yes. The Buddhists are also searching for this stone. They believe that it is worn by Avalokitesvara'

William then brought in the English perspective. 'Fair enough, All the religions have something to say about this stone. To add to the confusion, there is another version of the stone for which people had searched. It's called the Jacob's pillow. The Jacobites who wanted to re-establish the House of Stuarts on English throne had given it to the Scottish kings. It was believed to have been kept at the base of the Scottish throne. Once Scotland came under the English rule, some say that the Scots had given it to the English Monarchy. Now, it is in the Edinburgh Castle. Some say that the stone is a fake and is not of any importance.'

Vicky asked his questions 'It is said that Roerich had gifted this to the League of Nations. If it is so, then why has that world body failed? What happened to the other pieces? Did Roerich break them? How can Roerich place the stone in the cornerstone of Master building, at the same time donate it to the League of Nations?'

'These are excellent questions to solve this great unsolved mystery. The Cornerstone of Master Building is on the South West corner. In that location, there is a boiler room. In the year 1975, one guy by name Frank Horsch was found murdered in that room. He had come to discover the truth of the stone. It still remains an unsolved mystery as to who killed Frank Horsch.'

'I must pay a visit to this place' said Vicky.

'Take my advice. Be very careful. There have been stories of people getting beaten up for getting over curious around this subject. Someone is very touchy about this. Towards the end, even Wallace had doubts about Roerich. He was supposed to bring the Foundation stone of the New World to America. He could not convince anyone. After many doubts were raised about Roerich, he fell out of limelight. One day he angrily declared that he would take back the stone to the 'Ruler of World' in the Himalayas to unite this stone with the Mother stone. He claimed to have connection to the heavenly world called the Shambhala in Himalayas. Even Blavatsky believed in this notion. Nobody knows if he had reached Shambhala. Some say that he gave it to a Monastery in Tibet.'

'But why would anyone be interested to protect a hoax?'

'What you call as a hoax has very deep repercussions to the Secret societies. Things are not as simple as they seem Vicky. You will be shocked if you knew how this country was based on concepts that any god fearing person would shudder to even imagine.'

Jenny walked towards them and interrupted. 'Sorry to interrupt. The Professor wants you to analyze the lab report and prepare to answer some questions the Press might ask tomorrow.'

'Yes. If you will excuse me, Mr. William.'

'Sure. Go ahead Vicky. If you have any questions, call me on this number. William gave him his card'

'Thank you sir' Vicky shook his hand and left.

CHAPTER: TWENTY THREE

There have been many powerful stones that emerged out of India. Most of them belonged to the ruling king. There was a certain Syamantaka Mani, which generated enough Gold every day to feed a nation. There was another such powerful stone Chandra Mani which made the possessor to revel in permanent state of ecstasy. Another stone going by the name Indranila Nilamani, a dark blue Sapphire that had the potential to make human into divine, is the core of the wooden idol of Puri temple in Jagganath. Incidentally, the English word 'Juggernaut' originates from the word Jagannath because the huge chariot on which the deity is taken on a procession once a year is drawn without halt on its scheduled path. Compared to all the stones which had divine origins, the stone of Chintamani is considered as the most sought after. Other stones may give the possessor one specific power. Chintamani bestows divine power. Secret societies believed that their Gods originated from Sirius star. They believed that Chintamani originated from Sirius and had divine powers. Many legends spoke of the stone being broken. Some ventured to obtain the outer cover that was in shape of a cup. These pursuits were overshadowed by the Holy Grail stories which focused on a cup in which Jesus had the last Supper.

Ancient Legends speak volumes about Chintamani. The possessor of this stone could become immensely powerful physically, mentally and had the power to control nature. He gains the power to look into the past, gain knowledge on all the subjects. He becomes invincible. Legends also carry the story of it being broken. Hindu mythology speaks of it being worn by the Demon king, Ravan and he was killed by Ram only after Ram smashed Chintamani into pieces. The pieces and the core stone passed from generation to generation. Since 3,000 B.C, it is believed to be somewhere in the Himalayas. Some like the Russian Painter Roerich claimed it be in the possession of the God in the mystic place of Shambala. Some say it is in a secret Tibetan Monastery and the only reason China attacked Tibet was to get hold of the stone. Some say that the stone was destroyed and that act dried up River Saraswati.

The test report on the stone at Rixton University was very vague. Although, it threw light on some of the aspects and chemical composition of the stone, it left most of the questions unanswered. The stone had shown unidentified elements. The report read

It mentioned the Element to be that of Transition metal with intermixed, micrometer-sized bands crystal habit. It had a Specific Gravity of 11 and the Mohs Hardness Scale of between 8.0 to 9.0. The toughness was above that of Octahedrite.

The chemical composition stated the known compounds of SixOy, Mg, and Olivine formed 40% of the stone and left the unknown elements of 60%. It had a refractive Index of 2.540 with a vitreous luster. It's a slightly green.

The Press kits and the notes were ready by evening. Jenny gave the Master file to the staff to prepare copies. No one realized that they had missed their Lunch. They went out and had Pizzas and Vicky retired to the room early. He opened his email inbox.

There was a serious note from his uncle. Vicky sent him a pacifying reply. There was a Facebook add request from Jenny. He added her. He checked his mail and there was a reply from Professor Sastry.

Lying on the bed, he placed the laptop on his chest and opened the Professor's mail.

'There is a version that when Michael fought with Lucifer and how this stone was on the head of Lucifer and how Michael broke the stone and how it fell onto the Earth in several pieces. They cannot accept the Indian epics such as Ramayana or Hinduism. So, they make up stories for everything that has some importance to their lives.

You also must be aware of the secret societies. In the United States, there are many devil worshippers. They conduct what is known as the Black Sabbath. They use the cross upside down in their secret churches. What actually started as small groups that refused to believe in Christianity have now become completely evil cults indulging in all types of vices? They follow the wrong path of Tantra although they are not aware of it.

Roerich was one of them. All these secret societies believed that their purpose will be actualized if they found the Holy Grail. Dan Brown in his book Da Vinci code had written about it. You have read it I believe. But, there are inaccuracies in that book. The Holy Grail these secret societies were searching for was not the cup that Jesus drank in the last supper. Just think about it. What significance should the cup has to these societies which in fact worshipped the woman?

The Holy Grail is just a misnomer. It's a clever decoy. These cults are interested in something that can give them super natural powers. They cannot do miracles like Jesus Christ. Jesus Christ was son of God and he was powerful and sacred. They want a short cut method to get such powers.

You and I know that this is possible only when one excels in spirituality and when one obtains Siddhis by awakening Kundalini power inside. They do not believe in these austere rituals and discipline. They rather selected the wrong method of worship to obtain these powers. In spite of hundreds of years in search, they could not achieve their goal. That is the reason for their frustration and that is the reason why they are after the Chintamani stone.

Next time you go out, look carefully. You will find so many pagan signs in the United States especially in Washington D.C. The entire Government, Military and the Trade are infiltrated with people who are members of these societies.'

Vicky had to make an effort to process the information. In this mind, he wondered, Someday, this Professor will go to jail for expressing such views.

Since three days, he had so much on intake that he decided to take a break and watch a movie. He can start thinking about the stone at night, to get the right perspective.

He had fervently hoped that Professor Sastry would help him learn more about the Chintamani stone in a scientific manner. More than a man of Science, Sastry seemed to be a sensationalist and a person who comes out with the most bizarre theories. But, what is so wonderful about this person is that he has compelling answers that seem to carry conviction.

He opened his notes and jotted down everything he had assimilated in the past couple of days. Professor Chris had given him the honor to sit on the dais and give a statement apart from answering the questions fielded by the Press the following day. He set aside a Dark Green suit for the occasion.

CHAPTER: TWENTY FOUR

Sunil Rao was about to leave his desk when his editor called him.

'You better look into this Sunny. This should interest you' he pushed the fax paper on the table. It was the invitation for Press conference from Rixton University.

Sunil Rao or Sunny as he is known in the journalistic circles has penchant for occult and super natural subjects. A hardcore buff of 'The X-files', his one bed room apartment in Edison was filled with the X—files merchandize. Sunny had many times thought of quitting his job and getting into psychic reading. He had developed a heightened consciousness. What he had perceived initially as a gift is increasingly becoming a liability to him.

Born to a migrant family from India, Sunny joined the swelling ranks of peculiar species named as 'ABCD' or 'American Born Confused Desi' This species gets caught between the Indian and the American culture. The world they see in their schools, colleges and offices is entirely different from what they see and get taught at home. Eventually, they end up getting mental complexes or giving their parents complexes. In Sunny's case, his parents were happy that he believed in Gods, to be precise, Hindu Gods and that he has no intention to marry a 'Gori' or an 'American white skinned girl'.

Sunny was aware of the legend of Chintamani. But, he was convinced that this press conference would be a waste of time. The only Chintamani if at all exists, it should be somewhere in the Himalayas. Journalism taught him that 'without fire, there is no smoke' But again it also taught him the truth in famous dictum of President Reagan 'Trust, but verify.'

Concealing his indifference, he replied 'Sure Chief. I will attend'

Driving home in his battered car, Sunny pondered about the kind of questions he is going to ask. His newspaper NJ State Express, does not command the kind of stature which powerful ones such as New York Times, Wall Street Journal, Washington Post or New York Post do.

He decided to spend the rest of evening on the internet, gathering as much information as he can on the stone.

Next day Sunny arrived at the venue early. He saw Vicky and introduced himself. They sat down to talk.

On the dais were name plates. Right in the center was Prof. Chris Conrad. Seated to his left was Prof. Dietrich. Vicky had the slightest ideas who he was. To his right was his name Vikram Reddy. Towards his left was Prof. Ramos. The door burst open and the professor walked in along with a short bald man who had raised eye brows.

'Professor this is Vicky. Vicky, this is Professor Dietrich, The head of the Chemistry department.'

'Pleasure professor' But the professor did not show any sign of pleasure.

'So, you want me and the rest of the world to believe in the weird stuff you have said on this stone?'

'Excuse me?' Vicky was bewildered.

'Listen Son, There is nothing called Chintamani Stone. Just as there is no Philosopher's stone or the Holy Grail or the Fountain of Youth or the Jacob's pillow or the . . . .'

Vicky turned towards Prof. Chris and interrupted taking a serious note 'Excuse me professor. Unless it is proven otherwise, we have every reason to believe that the object found was the Chintamani stone. We had also found a plank with the letters clearly written on it'

Prof. Chris calmly replied. 'Precisely Vicky, As a man of Science and reason, I want to give you and Dietrich an equal and fair opportunity to prove what that object or stone really is'

'Sir, But is it apt to do so in the glare of the media?' Vicky hated sensationalism. He knew how a famous monk, a Great soul who had attended the Parliament of Religions in the year 1895 in Chicago was ridiculed and mocked and how he had to prove again and again the greatness of Hinduism and the validity of the truths of the religion. He was not that monk—Swami Vivekananda, who had proven the greatness of Hindu religion to the world. He was just Vicky.

Prof. Chris asserted 'No. Vicky. You are not going to fight. You are going to read your statement and he is going to read his. You will answer the questions posed to you and he will do the same. We are yet to arrive at conclusions and this is just a preliminary Press conference, almost a Press release.'

Vicky felt a pang of cramp in his tummy. The least he wanted now was an argument. He silently took his notes and sat on the chair.

Half an hour later the Press conference started. Professor Chris Conrad had arranged a presentation.

'Good Afternoon Ladies & Gentleman' he began and as is his style, jumped into the subject. As the lights dimmed, the focus of everyone shifted to the screen.

'Couple of weeks ago deep in the jungles of Mexico, Professor Ramos and his team had discovered an ancient temple'. The screen showed a temple what looked like a replica of Chichen Itza.

'This temple had a secret passage which opened when the professor pressed his hand on the turtle figure.' He showed the image of Kurmavatara—the idol of Vishnu's incarnation of a giant turtle to support the Mount Meru which was used to churn the Milky Ocean.

The next slide exhibited the char colored object and a dusty gold plank. 'This is the object or the stone that is the focus. The plank here is made out of solid gold. The letters inscribed on it are 'Chintamani Rahasya' written in Sanskrit. There are images of temples on it'.

The next slide showed the stone in its entire splendor. 'This is the actual stone that was hidden inside the char colored sheath'.

Then the lights brightened. 'I believe that this is a stone that has peculiar characteristics. This has certain unknown elements and it has some electro-magnetic properties.'

'Now, I introduce you to my distinguished colleagues Professor Dietrich—Head of the department of

Chemistry, Vikram from University of Madras, Chennai, India and expert in History, anthropology, religion and the emerging Noetic Science and Professor Ramos of University of Mexico. They will make their comments after which we will take the questions'

Dietrich cleared his throat and began 'The stone that is discovered is a piece of Moldavite. This is nothing but a remnant of a Meteorite that hit the Earth millions of years ago specifically in Croatia. Pieces of it had fallen in other countries. In ancient days, special powers were attributed to everything that comes from a distant land. Someone would have taken it to Mexico to earn name and fame and con the local Mexicans mixing it with their religious beliefs' He leaned over and looked indignantly at Vicky. Then he concluded 'I have nothing more to add. Any questions?'

'Can we see the actual stone and the plank?' one reporter asked.

Prof. Chris intervened 'Yes. You can. Let the camera focus on the display box and switch on the lights over it'

In a few seconds the screen was dazzling with shimmering light of white and light Green. Everyone present was awe struck by the powerful stone. Then another reporter asked 'If it was just a piece of Moldavite, then what makes it so special? We heard about the damage this thing had caused to your servers and electrical systems. Can you explain that?'

'I can't comment on it. There is nothing special about this stone in my opinion except that it has some elements unknown so far to the modern science'

'Would that not make it a special stone professor?' Sunny asked in a loud voice.

'Just because we do not know it fully does not make it special. We will crack the puzzle very soon'

'Then how can you call it Moldavite? Because the chemical composition of Moldavite is already known' Sunny persisted.

The Professor was taken aback by this. 'Yeah, It's a special type of Moldavite'

Sunny was annoyed by his arrogance and denial. 'You mean like Diamond is a special type of Coal? When can we get some definite answers Professor?'

'Science is not a monkey business. We believe in something only when it is proven empirically, unlike a few who has a fairy tale to tell. I have nothing more to say. My department will continue to work on it.'

CHAPTER: TWENTY FIVE

Prof. Chris then asked Vicky to speak. Vicky was not prepared for the onslaught of Dietrich. In fact, he was of the opinion that the Rixton University had not received any satisfactory answers from the Chemistry department and no one could explain the strange phenomenon. Upon suggestion from a Noetic Science researcher, Vicky was called all the way from India. He glanced at the crowd. Seated in the first row were Jenny, Akila and Prof. Ramos. He was surprised that he did not choose to sit on the dais although there was a seat for him there.

He understood that the notes prepared by him were of no use. He pulled the microphone towards him and started

'Good afternoon Ladies and Gentlemen. First, I would like to thank Prof. Chris and the Rixton University for giving me this opportunity to study and solve the mystery behind the discovery. Second, I would like to ask Prof.

Ramos who made the discovery in the first place to join me on the dais. Let us give him applause.' Everyone clapped as Prof. Ramos got on to the dais and sat beside Vicky.

All eyes were on Vicky now. 'Religion begins where Science ends. But Science begins to understand and talk when Religion had said it all. Science asks why? And Religion answers Why not? Many people in the West were generous enough to credit me with the title of a Lunatic and some with excessive brain cells even called me a fairy tale teller' he briefly looked at Dietrich. There was some laughter.

'Trust me. In the literary circles of high religion and science in India, they call me a non-believer and a blasphemous iconoclast'

Rising both his hands animatedly, Vicky continued 'Science and Religion are like two hands. You need both to get the job done—the job of finding the Truth. You say Newton discovered the concept of Gravity. I say that this was known at least 200,000 years ago to the Hindus. They called it as Aakarshan shakti. You say that science has discovered about atoms, germs and cells. These concepts were known to the ancient Hindus. It's all written in the texts along with proper nomenclature. Science talks about the positive and negative polarities. The concept of dualism was understood by ancient Hindu seers. Science is now struggling to understand the String theory stating the ten dimensions of the Universe and its functioning.

Hindus knew this reality hundreds of thousands of years ago. They also knew the dynamics of these dimensions and how they functioned. Every matter is a form of energy. The Hindu texts talk about the ten forms of 'Shakti' or the ten dimensions of Energy in Sri Maha Vidya. There are so many instances. It is of no doubt that certain physical substances are filled with positive energy and some with negative energy. We humans use only 8 percent of our brains potential. If we unlock this unused potential, we become very powerful. We can manipulate the physical world with our thoughts. Lab experiments have proven this. Our thoughts have power and they can influence outcomes in lives. The stone which Dietrich referred to as Moldavite is indeed a powerful stone. This has the capacity to empower Pineal gland.'

Vicky paused and drank some water and resumed.

'At the back of the neck there is a gland called Pineal gland. It secretes Melatolin, a hormone that maintains the rhythm of sleep and dreaming. This gland is larger in size in children. which is why they are imaginative? This gland vibrates or shivers whenever there is a spiritual experience or an experience of positive energy. Some believe that if this vibration is prolonged it leads to the opening of the third eye between the eye brows. If one meditates on this gland thoroughly, it takes the person to higher levels of consciousness and perceives higher truths. This stone can empower the person who holds it and it helps the process of apotheosis—transformation of Man into a God. And when I say God, I mean the power to control the physical world and the events. Noetic science is making strides to better understand this phenomenon.'

There was absolute silence except for the clicks of cameras. 'We live in this planet not by chance but by design. We humans are the essential part of the Universe. Everything is precisely ordained by the nature. For instance, it takes our Sun 25,920 years to pass through all the signs of the Zodiac. It is exactly equal to the number of times we breath in a single day. We have forgotten to perceive the influence of physical world on us. We have forgotten to understand the effect planets have on us. Because we have hardened ourselves with only 'reason' and what is beyond 'reason' is conveniently termed as 'non-science' or simply 'nonsense'.

The ancient man had a vegetative consciousness. He allowed the forces of nature flow through him. He understood the Nature and felt a part of it. He knew that Venus had influence on the copper content in his Kidneys.

He felt the ecstasy of full Moon and the dullness of a new Moon, as the waxing and waning of the Moon directly affected the expansion and contraction of pineal gland. That was the reason why the Hindus had associated the Moon as the ruler of Mind. Moon is also identified with Rice or Annam which has the life-giving force.

In the plant world, certain tubers were seen to grow rapidly during the Full moon day. In animal world, it is observed that the oysters increase and decrease in tandem with the Moon's waxing and waning. In the physical world it is common knowledge that Moon's gravitational force affects the waves of the ocean.

That is the reason why we must respect religion. That is why we must keep our minds open and not be narrow minded. A true man of Science does not shut his mind to any eventuality. That is why; we must give benefit of doubt to everything we come across. In this perspective, let me bring in the subject of the stone. This stone has the power of rapidly evolving human into a super-human. It has the power to make him obtain super natural powers. The only stone that is known to our ancient seers with such a quality is 'Chintamani' and as I have experienced the power of this stone personally. I would have hesitated to call it as 'Chintamani' if I had not found the plank with the words 'Chintamani Rahasya' written in Sanskrit on it. If you don't like the word, call it whatever you like to call it.

There are images of ancient temples on it with some symbols. It will take some time for us to figure out the meaning behind these symbols and images of the temples. Right now, I am on that job. You may ask questions now'

There was a barrage of questions. Vicky had a tough time answering some of them.

Sunny finally asked 'How much time will it take for the world to know the meaning of Chintamani Rahasya. We also want to see how the power of this stone works. When can we do that?'

Vicky replied 'I cannot put a timeline on it. We will keep you updated if we find something worthy to inform. The demonstrations of the powers of the stone will only be more appropriate after we first ascertain the secret behind it'.

The Press conference ended. Dietrich walked out silently Vicky stayed back and had an informal chat with some press persons and the other faculty of the University, who wanted to know more about his research and the amazing things he had said in his speech. Many television networks wanted an interview with him. He found it hard to give his contact information to everyone, as he had exhausted his name cards. So he gave them his email id.

CHAPTER: TWENTY SIX

Vicky pulled out his iPod and the speakers set and placed it carefully on the basin mantle, before turning the shower on. He played his favorite album of a collection of Western Classical music on his iPod. He had with him the best compositions of Beethoven, Mozart, Tchaikovsky, Bach, Vivaldi and Brahms.

After the shower, he reached over to read the latest of Sidney Sheldon.

Sipping on Pepsi, he wondered how this great author's works captured the imagination of generations of readers, as he always maintained the protagonist as a lady. The powerful image of a woman had been always been the undercurrent of human psyche. Almost all the secret societies have kept a woman as their object of prayer. They believed her to be the source of strength. Sufism which is an amalgamation of Hinduism and Islam

151

also believed that without the grace of Pari—or a lady angel, there cannot be any spiritual enlightenment. The Christians believed in the power of Mother Mary. The Buddhists particularly in China believed that the prayers to Kwan Yin or Gwan Yin, the feminine form of Buddha or Avalokitesvara bring fortune and health. Ancient Greeks, Romans, Egyptians and Scythians prayed female Goddesses.

The Hindus believe in the power of Mother Goddess. The entire religion revolved around Mother Shakthi and Lord Shiva. She is the originator of the Universe. In her are the good and evil. Nothing is beyond her and nothing is above her. Praying to her, releases the human from all bondages and weaknesses. A devotee of Mother Goddess fears nothing.

All the positive and negative energies are inside her. She can make a human go mad after vices and deny him the virtues. And those who are given the virtues must be careful not to take pride in them. If they do so, they lose them over a period of time, as taking pride in virtues itself is a vice. It leads to false ego. A perfect person is one who is completely egoless. Such a person gets the blessings of Shiva and nothing can stir him.

Mother Goddess or Devi Goddess also has the negative side or the ferocious side. Without the destructive power, there cannot be regeneration. The Hindus pray to Mother Kali—the one that determines the time and whose time has ended. She is the first dimension of the Universe.

There are many aspects of this Shakti or Universal power. Some pious sages had the ability to bring out and define the positive manifestations of Shakti such as Gayathri manifested first by Sage Viswamitra.

Similarly there are evil occultists who evoke the most negative aspects of this Universal Power. They invoke the power of Shakini, Dakini and the likes to reach their evil goals. No matter how much they yearn to gain powers, they are defeated in the hands of the pious ones who get their power from the Supreme Mother.

These realities are not confined to the Hindus. Ancient tribes from Australia and New Zealand to the deep jungles of Africa and Amazon have prayed to Mother Goddess. The names and forms vary. Similar to the Hindus they also had evil men aspiring to gain powers for materialistic ends. Ancient Phrygians prayed to Cybele—the terrifying aspect of Mother Goddess. Her devotees went into such a rage that they cut off their testicles.

Breaking his thoughts, he resumed reading, eating chips and sipping Pepsi. After bath, he opened his laptop and found a mail from Prof. Sastry. There was a mail from his Uncle expressing his happiness that Vicky is going to visit him over weekend. There were four requests for interviews from the press. He did not have enough energy to go through the details of Sastry's mail. He slept for two hours.

He was ready for Jenny who picked him up. Vicky anticipated her to take him someplace in New Jersey. But she had plans to take him to the Park Avenue Hotel in New York. She liked the exquisite dining at its restaurant Silver leaf Tavern. En route, Jenny asked him about his life.

First they danced to couple of waltz numbers. Jenny felt very comfortable with him. He was very gentle and well mannered. She forgot for once their professional relationship and their unspoken friendship. For her, it was getting something more special then friendship. They danced for half an hour. Then they decided to move to the table and order food.

Silver leaf Tavern is a gourmet delight. She ordered Buffalo wings and he preferred Fish and Chips. Vicky ordered Pepsi and she ordered white wine. They discussed about the press conference.

On the way back, Jenny asked about Hinduism. Vicky explained. 'Ever since Max Muller had translated Rig Veda and other Hindu texts, students of Western theology focused their attention on Hinduism. From these translated works, Western philosophers and religious scholars could unsolve the mysteries of their own religions. Hinduism was the oldest and the deepest religion of mankind. He also explained how some selfish people of knowledge had tampered with this religion and just as all other religions was subjected to dogma and orthodox rites.

It was late when Jenny dropped him at his room. She walked along with him to his room. Vicky offered her to stay back a while and have some coffee. They spent an hour chatting. Both of them found it difficult to say Good bye. This was the first time Vicky had taken interest in a girl. He then informed her that he would be leaving the next day morning to spend time with his uncle in Edison. So, he would only see her on Monday afternoon.

Jenny looked a bit disappointed. She had fallen in love with Vicky. She did not even think for a moment that she needed to check with him if he had other plans. She took it for granted that she was the only one Vicky knew and she was the only one who would take him around. Somehow, she felt he belonged to her.

Vicky made it more awkward saying 'It is very late Jenny. I think you better go and catch some sleep'.

CHAPTER: TWENTY SEVEN

Next morning, Vicky called Professor Chris and briefed him about his plans for the following week. He gave the phone number of his uncle Sagar where Vicky would be spending that day through the weekend. The Professor was clearly unhappy. Ever since the news broke about the stone, his department was inundated with calls from all the sections of society. Churches, Research Labs, Corporations, and Newspapers that missed the Press meet some brotherhood organizations and even an eccentric Tantrik who claimed that it belonged to him and that it was stolen.

He wanted Vicky to answer most of the sane questions. But, as it was almost weekend, he asked Vicky to take a break, but asked him to decipher the images and text on the plank. Vicky signed on the register and carried the carefully packed plank with him.

A few minutes later, he was sitting in a plush Lexus car with his Uncle at the wheel.

'So, how is your work going on?' asked his uncle.

'It's exciting. We are about to unlock one of the mysteries of ancient world'

'Oh yeah, What is it?'

'It's about the stone called Chintamani. It was found in Mexico and I am trying to ascertain the secret behind it.'

'Will that make you famous?'

'I am not here to get famous uncle. I am here to solve something. That is my job. I am not interested in being famous'

'So, you have not changed a bit, even after coming to America?'

'Nothing will change me, uncle. I am what I am. Man should earn money and Money should not earn Man'

'Now, even if you had come here in a normal Ford, you would be the same person that I know. Driving a Lexus does not make you another person'

'Are you a communist?' his uncle was irritated.

'No'

'Then stop being so cynical. People respect me as I had worked hard to reach the position where I am in life today'

'Yes. I agree. But what if you were a rich kid who got this from your Dad's inheritance? Does it show on the rear of your car that you had worked hard for it?

'My God, You are impossible. Your wife will have a tough time with you.'

There was some uncomfortable silence. Vicky said 'Uncle. You know how I hate these pretentious show offs. I hate people who flaunt wealth, power and connections. Why is it that people cannot raise above these petty aspects? Don't they know that whatever they earn is not going to go along with them when they die?'

'Now Vicky, Stop talking likes a monk. I should blame your mother for bringing you up in this fashion'.

'There is nothing wrong with her or me uncle. It is this society that is all so narrow minded and cheap'

'Who are you to judges how the Society must behave?'

'I am entitled to have my own opinion' Vicky snapped back.

'Let us not spoil our moods. In a few hours Rachana and her parents are visiting us. They will have dinner before they leave. Now, don't scare the poor little girl with your outlandish communist philosophy'

'Communist philosophy? Oh, Never mind uncle. I will discuss American Football with her'

For a man who had touched the shores of America with less than a hundred dollars in his pocket, his uncle had made quite a fortune. His sprawling house and a huge garden with pool looked swanky. He had four luxury cars in his stable. His aunt was at the doorstep and welcomed Vicky warmly. He was surprised that they had hired a couple as servants. They were Indians but were elderly couple. Vicky did not allow the elderly person to carry his large bag.

'I will carry it myself' he said.

In his room he carefully unpacked the box and took out the gold plank. As the drapes were kept open the natural sunlight hit the plank and the images on it such as pictures of some temples, some sea dragons and some unusual markings gained clarity.

Vicky hated to believe in certain omens. This was a contradiction he was unable to overcome. He usually dismissed many superstitions. But, his personal experience had taught him to believe in certain psychic phenomena that gave him a premonition of what was about to come.

Whenever his left eye twitched, he went through a bad phase. Whenever his right eye twitched, he got good news. Since Sunday morning, his left eye had been twitching almost uncontrollably. This meant something bad was on the horizon. He went into a bout of depression suddenly.

If he hated anything the most about himself, it was his depression. At such instances, he lost interest in everything. He lost enthusiasm to work which he found worthless. He questioned the need to lead a life when someday he is going to die. The entire world and his life seem to be pretentious and farcical.

One side effects of his depression is his uncontrollable temper. He lost temper very easily. People, who knew him well, never provoked him at such times. Violent temper had been a denominator in many a genius such as Beethoven. Depression was a characteristic of Tchaikovsky and Van Gogh. But, Vicky was not as brilliant as those magnificent personalities. He was just an expert on certain subjects and a spiritually evolved person. In this world of comparisons, brilliance is always a relative concept.

One secret which he never shared with anyone including his parents was that he believed to be overpowered by a negative emotion that made him consider everything in life and the world as pretentious and meaningless. He felt shortness in breath and difficulty in speech. His mind resisted prayer. His mind ceased to torment, only when he meditated intensely. After a few minutes, the negativity would seep into him again. During such periods, he preferred darkness to light, silence to music, and coldness to warmth.

However, he overcome such thoughts with the help of meditation and yoga.

Now he cannot afford to be in this state of mind, considering the enormity of task ahead of him. He filled the basin with cold water and immersed his head into it and blanked his mind for a few moments. He felt his body shaking for a few times. It was as though the negativity was exorcised.

He was served lunch. He relished the home cooked food. Then, everyone got busy making arrangements for Rachana's family to arrive.

He resumed reading his Sidney Sheldon book and dozed off. Vicky was woken up by his aunt.

'Get up. They are here'

'Who'

'Rachana and her parents'

Vicky suddenly felt out of sorts. He went to the bathroom and washed his face and put on some Cologne.

After the formal introductions, Vicky and Rachana went into the garden for a chat. Vicky told her that he was not mentally prepared to get married. He said he needed more time to reach that state of mind. He said that they can remain as friends. She appreciated his frankness. They spoke about their lines of work.

Vicky suddenly felt his head reeling.

'Are you okay Vicky' Rachana inquired 'Oh My God, you are bleeding through your nose'.

Vicky collapsed and hit the ground. She shrieked.

After couple of hours, Vicky found himself in a Hospital. The doctors said Vicky suffered from exhaustion, but could not explain the nose bleeding. They presumed it to be a mild skin rupture.

Dr.Rachana insisted that he got brain scan taken. Vicky remembered the scan he had taken back in Chennai before he flew to the United States. The report was lying at the diagnostic center. He was not interested to know the result. He feared there was something seriously wrong.

He was sent home and was advised rest for a day. He was relieved that his family did not get panicky. Thankfully no one called his parents.

Vicky dozed off on his bed and woke up well past dinner time.

CHAPTER: TWENTY EIGHT

He went into the kitchen and poured out cold chocolate milk in a large glass and sat at the work table to review the notes. He focused on the plank repeatedly for clues. He suspected that as the letters were engraved in Sanskrit, he must refer to the ancient Hindu texts for the key to decode the images.

One of the two references for Geography in ancient texts was Kishkintha Kanda of Ramayana the Hindu epic. In this, Sugreeva the king of apes educates those who were bound to search for Sita on the Geography of the planet. Westerners always had difficulty in accepting the fact that the world that they had discovered recently was very much known to the ancient Hindus.

Sugreeva had mentioned about Java and the seven kingdoms to the east. He identified the lands of Tin mines and gives their accurate direction and distance which is

165

present-day Myanmar. He also mentioned the Silver mines presumably Argentina. He also warmed about the kind of wild animals in these regions.

He cautioned them not to visit two specific regions in the sea that are in triangular shape on either side of the planet on the same latitude. India has the world's best astrologers and seers. Like Nostradamus, a Great Indian Saint Potuluri Veera Brahma made many accurate predictions about the world and mostly about India.

In the modern days, accurate astrological predictions are made by a very few. One great astrologer in India who is not only reputed for making accurate astrological predictions but also who can give explanation to some of the world's unsolved mysteries is Mulugu Ramalingeswara Vara Prasad. He is renowned highly and is the most sought after expert in the field of astrology.

The modern world knows them as the Dragon Triangle and the Bermuda Triangle. The Dragon Triangle south of Japan is the area of influence for Planet 'Rahu' and exactly opposite side of Earth, the Bermuda Triangle near the Caribbean is the area of influence attributed to Planet 'Ketu'. This fact was unknown, until the astrologer Mulugu from India explained the phenomenon in detail.

These two serpentine shadow planets of Indian astrology are the forces in the ocean that pulls down anything that passes over it. Vicky identified two rough triangles on the plank that helped me to draw the co-ordinates easily.

166

The other reference book is Padma Puran in which a clear description of the world is given. It mentions about the Sea dragons and also the land of the great eagle, the tin mines and the silver mines. This book was forbidden to be read anytime. It was meant to be read only when someone in the family died. Vicky did not believe in such restrictions. He was a rebel. He accessed his scanned copy of the book from his Kindle e-book reader.

Juxtaposing the ancient knowledge to the plank gave Vicky a clear idea about the places that were on the plank. The markings and temple images engraved on it indicate that perhaps either pieces of Chintamani or information related to that are placed in these places. He set out to work on each temple, studying its location using a scale ruler and co-related the place on the world map.

Next morning, his uncle dropped him at the University with a warning to take things easy. As he approached the security, he noticed many Police cars flashing lights and their wireless phones crackling.

'Vicky, Something terrible has happened' Akila tapped his shoulder and spoke in trembling voice. She was in a state of shock.

The place was filled with Policemen and in a distance he saw Prof. Chris with his hands on his head. He looked at Vicky.

'What the hell happened?' asked Vicky

'Jenny is dead Vicky. Someone had beheaded her'. Akila broke down.

Vicky's head started reeling. His mind could not process what he just heard. His brain went numb and mechanically he asked

'What? What are you talking about?' He almost fainted and taking support of a desk he leaned over it and shook his head.

He shut himself to the outside world. Jenny's face came to his mind. He lost sense of time and space.

'Vicky' the voice was very loud. He turned back to see a burly officer looking daggers at him.

'Yes'.

'Come with me.' He turned back.

Vicky followed him. Akila held his hand 'Are you alright Vicky?' He did not answer.

In the room the Police officers were talking to Prof. Chris.

Vicky reached for the glass of water and asked 'What happened?'

'Someone killed Jenny this morning. Someone had beheaded her and the Chintamani stone is missing' the professor said in a depressed tone.

CHAPTER: TWENTY NINE

The story of Chandra perhaps encapsulated all that has to be known about Hinduism. It gives the essence of all the holy scriptures and it reveals secrets that have been zealously guarded by many for hundreds of thousands of years. The path that he had chosen was the finest and the most noble to reach the ultimate state. Knowing and following this path can make anyone a saint, a super human who gets evolved from normal human being state to that of divine.

He began his new life with great enthusiasm under the kind guidance of his new Master, Vishwa Dharma. The other disciples were puzzled by the newcomer at their ashram. The Master had initiated Chandra into the sainthood with auspicious rites.

It is universally held that using water for religious purposes originated with Hinduism. This ritual spread throughout the world and every Secret society in Europe and America had used similar initiation methods. Water was required for the sacred rites of cleansing oneself from the sins or beginning a new life. In India, rivers are considered sacred and the most sacred of them was River Ganga or Ganges. Certain Hindu theology gurus argue that the idea of baptizing in Christianity had its origins in Hinduism.

The sacred chant of 'Mantra Pushpam' that has the repeated verses of 'Ya yevam veda, Yo aapayatam veda, aayatanavaan bhavati' only explains the importance of water and is a text book lesson on Vishnu and rituals. It extols that the person who is in the know of this has known everything and thus is liberated. This simple collection of verses is often misused by the priestly class in India to fool the gullible and ignorant masses because the verses seem to be very 'Vedic'. They cheat the people who do not know the meaning of the verses by chanting them in every ceremony.

Chandra followed a strict regimen. He woke up at 4:00 in the morning. This time is called as 'Brahma Muhurtam' which is considered to be the most sacred time of the day. After performing daily ablutions, he sat down in nearby woods under a tree and mediated on the mantra or a scared hymn given by his Master. He meditated until noon and then he went to the ashram. He was given a piece of dried bread and a vegetable after which he would resume mediation in the court yard of the ashram until evening. In the evenings, he bathed again and recited the mantra and listen to his Master's sermons.

Chandra was troubled by visions of a Snake whenever he sat down for meditation. He consulted his Guru about this. Then, his Guru placed his hand on Chandra's head and that obstacle was removed from his psychic domain. His master said that Chandra suffered from an astrological predilection that put him in a difficult position from two shadow planets, Rahu and Ketu.

Rahu has the head of a Snake and body of a Man and Ketu has head of a Man and body of a snake. He was asked to appease both Rahu and Ketu by meditating and chanting their mantras. The snake has always been the obstacle to most of the realized souls. Be it the Buddha, Mahavira or Jesus, it has tried to obstruct their path. Whereas most of them have opposed and fought the Snake, Chandra due to the wisdom of his Guru, abnegated the karmic reason behind this. These two planets are propitiated indirectly by the Chinese by their adulation of Dragons. Most Chinese are free from the negative influences as the Dragon worship brings in good luck and fame, they believed.

Snake also has auspicious side in Hinduism. King Cobra is prayed to in the temples. God Vishnu had Adi Sesha the giant snake as his bed. When ancient temples wanted to safeguard precious wealth, the learned priests invoked the ferocious snake Takshak to guard the treasure. Everything in Hinduism has its importance and purpose, including the wild and the dangerous.

The recent findings of enormous wealth at Padmanabha temple brought a mystery into the lime light. The last treasury chamber could not be opened by the priests as they read a warning written on the door with symbols of snake that if the door was opened without the proper appeasement rituals, a great Tsunami would take place causing considerable damage. Only a learned priest could open it and no one could find such a learned priest and it remained closed.

Chandra's rituals went on for a few months. Then, the meditation became rigorous. Once Chandra found the strength to continue tapasya (meditation) on his own accord, he left the ashram and went into deep jungle and started to meditate. He ate only the fruits, roots and vegetables and drank the water from a nearby pond. He slowly cut down his food intake and spent day and night in meditation. Very soon, he forgot about the world around him and immersed himself in the meditation of Devi Mother Goddess.

His Kundalini, the serpentine spiritual energy in him awakened and the Chakras of his body got purified and energized. He felt tremendous energy fill his being from the bottom of his spinal cord to the top of his head called the Sahasrara Chakra.

The power of Kundalini is a dormant force lying at the base of spinal cord. According to Hindu ascetics, the physical body is superimposed by energy centers called the

Chakras. The imbalance in the Chakras, result in ailments both physical and mental.

For those in the path of serious meditation and pure heart, the Kundalini awakens. It is a force that can do harm than good if it is not properly channelized. To channelize this energy, one needed a true Guru, who should be a realized soul and who has the Kundalini power thoroughly realized. Vishwa Dharma, who Chandra had taken to be his Master or Guru, helped him.

After teaching Chandra the practice of meditation and tapasya, Vishwa Dharma taught him Raj Yoga—the most difficult and yet the highest form with which it is very easy to realize God. Raj Yoga involved a scientific process of using the mind itself as an instrument to understand the inner self and then to cleanse oneself of all the negative energies and obsessions or 'Vasanas' and to make oneself sacred and holy to imbibe Godly power by constantly meditating on God. These persons are usually unattached and are disinterested in the worldly activities.

Then Vishwa Dharma initiated Chandra into Shiva Yoga. It removed one's Karmic layers. As per the principle of Karma, every human being suffers due to his or her past deeds both in this life and previous births. If one had done good deeds, that person enjoyed luxuries, happiness and peace of mind in this life, But, even that status is not absolute and is subject to the deeds one does in the current life.

Vishwa Dharma narrated an example to explain this. There were two powerful spiritual personalities in India. They were the avadhootas or Godly persons—incarnations of God. Vishwa warned Chandra to bear in mind the difference between the Godly persons and the so called 'God men'

'God men are cheap tricksters. They are black magicians who gain powers and demonstrate them to the public and make money and earn fame. But Godly men are different. They absorb people's sins and misdeeds and show them the path. They solve their problems. Two such entities are Shirdi Sai Baba and Ramakrishna Paramahamsa'.

'Today, in India, every other Hindu house either has a photo of Shirdi Sai Baba or Ramakrishna. It is their divinity that is worshipped and even today their divine souls guide and help their disciples. There are many more Godly persons in India. But the reason I narrate these two is to explain the principle of Karma.'

Chandra listened with eagerness. 'When Ramakrsihna reached the final stages of salvation, he prayed to Mother Goddess to give him liberation. Liberation meant that his soul would be mingled into the divinity and it would no longer undergo the process of births and deaths. But, the Mother Goddess said to him that as he had done many good deeds, there is huge surplus of good karma and it has to be spent out before he rises above the karma trap. Then, Ramakrishna prayed to the Mother to transfer all the good karma to Shirdi Sai baba. Spiritual people communicate instantly through Telepathy. So, Shirdi Sai baba left his body in good care of one of his disciples and he entered the body of Ramakrishna and imbibed all the spiritual and good karma and then left the body and entered his own body. From that day onwards, the name and fame of Shirdi multiplied.'

Vishwa Dharma continued. 'You are destined for liberation or Moksha. You know that already. Whatever you do, just do it with a feeling of being just an instrument in hands of God. Nothing more, Then Karma principle would not apply to you'

As weeks and months rolled by, Chandra was initiated into Shambhavi Yoga and then he was asked to read many texts of Adi Sankaracharya. He was finally initiated into the Sri Vidya. Sri Vidya or Dasa Maha Vidya is considered to be the most powerful and ultimate spiritual practice in the Universe. It makes the person as powerful as the Universe. The knowledge of Dasa Maha Vidya is a very rare one known to only a few learned priests and holy men.

It contains the knowledge of the energy that permeates this Universe and it also gives the keys to unlock the energies and to clearly understand the manifestations and gain the cosmic power.

CHAPTER: THIRTY

Today the physicists struggle to understand the 'String theory' often dimension of the Universe. They 'discover' things that are known to the Hindus hundreds of thousands of years ago. Practitioners of Sri Vidya are aware that the entire Universe is comprised and is run by the dynamics of 10 grades of power which manifests themselves as 10 dimensions.

These 10 powers are manifestations of Mother Goddess who is aptly called as 'Shakti' or 'Power' She along with 'Shiva' the non-egoistic still consciousness form the entire Universe.

Many eastern philosophies emerged from this core concept. People who did not understand Hinduism or who were too narrow minded to understand it formed their own versions. Some of them called it at Ying and Yang. Everything that moves or has energy is part of

'Shakti' and everything that is absolute stillness of deep meditative bliss is 'Shiva'.

'Shakti' is better known as the Mother Goddess. All the positive, neutral and negative energies are in her. People who obtain the grace of her do not suffer from any cravings or desires in life. She is the creator of illusion. She is the creator of ignorance and knowledge. Without her grace, no spiritual progress is possible. Many people have destroyed their lives by setting out on spiritual path and falling prey to the passions of flesh and worldly attractions. They never realize that unless they have the grace of Mother Goddess, they can never overcome their mental weaknesses.

Vishwa Dharma narrated each and every aspect of the 10 Cosmic forces or the powers. Chandra must gain the grace of every one of these manifestations of 'Shakti', before setting out on this path independently.

'There are two types of Tanta practice—Dakshina and Vama. Dakshina is the proper Vedic manner to meditate on the positive manifestations of Mother Goddess. This is a very grueling method as the meditation must target on the powers that are on the highest planes of Shakthi. There are forces that exist even very close to the Human plane.

These forces are much easier to communicate with. But, as easy they are to propitiate they do not let you move ahead in your spirituality. One easily succeeds in making these forces do things for you. But, the day you do not satisfy them, they harm you and leave you.

Foolishly, some people attributed these low level forces to even Village Goddesses. One must be careful not to confuse the evil forces with village goddesses. They are both different. A Village Deity is a benevolent incarnation of Mother Goddess. These deities exist in the lower planes of consciousness and thus are easily approachable to the common men. They help and protect the people and also show their wrath if they are treated with disrespect. In Southern India, often you will find a temple built on the outskirts of the village for these Goddesses.

On the other hand, evil forces are manifested by Vama Tantra and they are propitiated for wealth and trickery. The devotee of such evil forces engages in most ghastly acts. At nights, they choose a lonely place either a burial or cremation ground or a forest. They bring along with them a woman of low character and engage in grossest forms of copulation with them. The practitioner makes a geometrical diagram of the evil deity and then offers it liquor, meat and also the sacrifice of a goat or a chicken. He then engages in grotesque acts with the woman and he assumes to have obtained the spiritual power as he thinks of himself as Shiva and the woman as Shakti and that he is drawing the power of spirituality from her body into his. In fact, the Buddhists in later stages of deterioration have adapted this form of Tantra and even today many Chinese forms of Buddhism believe that by doing such acts, a Person becomes very powerful as he draws the power from a woman. These disgusting acts do not have any scientific proof and yet they are popular due to their gross nature. These practitioners end up satisfying the evil forces who obey them or give them certain powers to mesmerize people. They show magic tricks to the gullible and then snatch their money and eventually become prosperous and lead luxurious lives.'

'Master, what is the purpose of such activities? The practitioner could earn the same by leading the life of a householder'.

'It is the short-cut method without the need to follow the rules of the society. These men get away with everything and anything. Often, they victimize people and using their tantric powers, they put up a show. For a common man, a miracle performed is enough to believe that the performer is equal to God and so he obeys him no matter what. That is why it is attractive path for the bad and evil'.

'Dakshina Tantra also involved geometrical designs. These designs or models are called the Yantras. A Yantra is the store house of spiritual energy. The triangles, circles and lotus petal designs on a yantra suggest the manifestation of certain form of Mother Goddess. It can be three dimensions or two dimensions. It is also called as 'Sri Yantra' or 'Sri Chakra' when you have the highest form of Mother Goddess. The Sri Chakra is the most potent and the most powerful yantra and it represents the exact dynamics of Shakti. As I said there are different forms of Yantras for the ten different forms of Shakti'

'Master, then each form of Shakti also must have its own Mantra or the prayer'

'Yes. Each form of Shakti has its own Yantra, the diagram, Mantra, the prayer and Tantra, the method. Each form of Shakti blesses the practitioner with powers. Once the practitioner succeeds in obtaining the grace and blessings of the ten forms of Shakti, he is well prepared to obtain liberation at any time. Such persons can also select the time of their death'

CHAPTER: THIRTY ONE

Vishwa Dharma brought ten books and lay before Chandra.

'Here are the 10 books that explain about each cosmic force, the method of worship and all the information. You must read each book carefully and understand the aspects before meditating. If you succeed in this, then you can be rest assured that there is no force or power in the Universe that can harm you. You will raise above all the mental weaknesses. You will be able to sustain without food or water. You will not require any sleep or rest. You will gain control over time and space and objects. You will in fact evolve from a Human being to a Super Human Being'

Chandra listened with deep concentration.

'The first and the foremost of the ten forms of Shakti is 'Kali'. She is the master of 'Time'. She is the destroyer.

Unless the old is destroyed, there is no place for the new. She destroys ego, false pride, lacunae in humans. She destroys all the wrong things in a human being. She is the one who controls and manifests Time. The practitioner who prays to Kali is not afraid of death. Her form is very fierce with garland of skeletons and tongue stretched out. She has the head of a demon in her hand and stands on the body of a dead demon'

The second form is 'Tara'. She is responsible for transmitting the sound force with great speed. She answers to the devotees needs very rapidly. That is why she is prayed to in times of any danger at Sea by fishermen and vessel captains. She is also the one who guides and protects. She is associated with Avalokitesvara by the Buddhists. She is also known as 'Neela Saraswati' as she gives the divine knowledge to her devotees.

Now, I reveal to you the most powerful form of Divine mother. She is the epi-center of this Universe. Every form of Shakti has its own Shiva. But this form does not, because she sits on top of Shiva who sleeps. She is known as 'Lalita-Tripurasundari' The word Lalitha means playful. She is the source from which the entire Universe and all its beings and non-beings and all its Gods and Goddesses gain power. She is known as 'Tantrik Parvati' and when a devotee prays to her; he loses all the weaknesses and obsessions. The Divine Mother has a younger form by name 'Bala Tripura Sundari'. Practitioners who find it difficult to meditate on Divine Mother pray and obtain the blessings of 'Bala Tripura Sundari' She can be appeased with chanting of Lalitha Sahasranama—the thousand chants of Divine Mother Goddess.'

'What is the significance of Lalita Sahasranama Master?'

'This is the most powerful prayer to the Goddess. It is said that the knowledge of this must not be propagated as it will be put to misuse by the undeserving. The power it gives to the chanter is tremendous. If one prays to Mother Lalita meditating on her with background of Moon, he gains tremendous divine power. If he mediates and chants this sitting in front of the King's palace, the King would personally visit his place and offer him anything he asks for'.

'The next form is that of Bhuvaneshvari. There are 14 worlds and she is the commander or leader of all these worlds. Then there is Bhairavi who is a fierce Goddess. I must mention carefully here about Chinna masta, the next form of Devi. Her form is very horrific as she decapitates her own head and drinks the blood from the trunk. Below her feet are a man and woman in copulation. She signifies conquest of all desires and conquest of one's ego—decapitation. Then there is Dhumavati, the opposite of existence or emptiness. She is considered as the widow Goddess and yet she is worshipped as it is from the emptiness that this Universe came into existence. She is the balancing negative force'

'The next form is Bagalamukhi. She is the resisting force. She has a paralyzing affect on the enemies. Her preferred color is Yellow and her devotees wear Yellow color and pray to her. No matter how intelligent the opponent is, his mind freezes and his logic quit him temporarily'.

'Then you have another powerful manifestation called Matangi, the Prime Minister of Lalitha Tripura Sundari. She is blue in color. Praying to her, results in obtainment of all the Siddhis or occult powers. The final form of Devi is that of Kamalaatmika, She is the opposite force of Dhumavati. She is the provider of plentiful. She blesses her devotees with immense wealth and helps them fulfill their responsibilities preparing them for ultimate liberation. She is the same power as Mother Goddess Lakshmi'.

'Now, take this book and carefully read it. I have written it and I am giving it to you and not to any of the disciples here. I trust you will pass this penultimate stage of reaching the eternal state of bliss'

Chandra quietly took the scriptures and the books and paid respects to his Guru and left the place. For the next 5 years, he will put himself through extreme austerities.

CHAPTER: THIRTY TWO

Chandra went deep into the forest. After a few days, he stopped eating food and lived only on water. A few days later, he stopped drinking water too and completely immersed himself in meditation. For months he meditated on each form of the Divine Mother. After about 60 months, he reached his goal. He overcame all the obstacles in mind and then one day, he experienced massive surge of energy flowing in him and he had a vision of Mother Goddess.

He gained extreme spiritual powers and occult powers. He had the power to see the future and could understand people's problems. He mastered the power to manifest anything out of thin air. He could cure people and suggest solutions to their problems. After obtaining the divine powers, he went back to his Master. His Master was pleased with his disciple.

'Chandra. Now you have reached the penultimate stage of spirituality. The next step is to realize Godhood. It is very difficult to reach the stage which you have reached. Many people get tempted to use these powers to gain fame and fortune. I want to know from you if you also desire fame and fortune'

'Master, I do not seek either fame or fortune. Every moment now, I am rejoicing in the bliss of divinity. I cannot think of anything else'

'Good. But, you have a task ahead of you which would be of immense importance to the mankind. As you have not thought about your future, I want you to sit this afternoon and meditate on your future and it will reveal itself to you.'

'Yes Master'. Chandra that after noon, sat in deep meditation and his future opened up before him. All the important events, the place where he would migrate to, the people who would come to meet him, the actual purpose of his life are manifest before him. Slowly, coming out of meditation, Chandra decided to leave for the deeper side of the Himalayas the next day. He left his Master's place forever. He now communicated with his Master through telepathy.

He knew exactly the place where he had to spend rest of his life. It was a place with natural cave formations on one side and a few villages, couple of miles away. He saw a cave formation overlooking a lush green valley down. He selected a cave and continued his meditation, eating and sleeping very less.

A few miles behind the cave held secrets that a very few enlightened souls knew and understood its importance. Chandra was strong and achieved the heights of spiritual status at a very young age. He alone had the courage and the mental power to perform a task that would be of global significance.

A few villagers came in the morning to his cave and cleaned it. Womenfolk brought fresh water and left food for Chandra. He never spoke to anyone. When the children fell sick, the villagers brought them to Chandra and made them to touch his feet and in that very instance the crying stopped and they were miraculously cured.

The cave formation was on a plateau. In spite of the steep elevation, the villagers served Chandra and provided food for him every day. It was during winters that they found it difficult to climb the terrain. The village chief had requested Chandra several times to come and live in the village. But, Chandra was adamant.

'Please do not bother about me and my comforts. I can manage on my own'. Those were the only words he ever spoke.

Then the villagers hit on an ingenious idea. They found another cave at a distance and they cleared it to make a kitchen and living dwelling in it with a fire place. During winters, villagers took turns every week to stay in that cave and cook and serve Chandra. Although he did not require any heating, they kept his cave warm and lit a lamp with clarified butter in front of an image of Lord Shiva in his cave.

After a few years, his cranium on the skull split open and his spiritual energy went up in a fountain. Except for a handful of humans, this was an almost impossible task. In the recent memory, Ganapati Muni was the person who achieved this state. Chandra's head was now filled a glow, a magical aura. He was now fully prepared for the future.

Chandra became a household Guru for the villagers. They lead a happy life. Once, a youngster who lived in Delhi visited his native village. When he heard about the Holy sage, he first ridiculed the villagers for being so gullible. But, when he went to look at him, he fell on his feet. He wanted to take a photograph of Chandra. But, when he took it, he saw an eye blinding illumination around his body. Chandra had asked him to delete the image. He did not want people to worship him. This attitude separated the truly divine spiritual masters from the fake tantriks who were just fame and money mongers.

CHAPTER: THIRTY THREE

The Department of Public Safety at Rixton University was called in initially the moment Akila found the gruesome dead body of Jenny. The detective on duty soon followed the procedure and called in the officers from the Rixton Police Department. In a matter of minutes the entire area was cordoned off and the forensics was called in.

In the meantime, the chief of police had ordered Detective Mitchell Johnson to lead the case. Mitchell is a cool headed officer with a deep analytical mind. Intelligent and hard working, he was a role model for his colleagues. He had solved many difficult cases. Had he lived in the New York City, he would have been an ideal officer for the NYPD. But, in a relatively crime free area where petty crimes were usual, the beheading of a Researcher at the University had become a high profile case.

The Press was there already and Mitchell had that morning tried to connect things and understand what exactly happened and the motive behind the murdered.

'I want to have a look at the Surveillance Cameras' he said

'Unfortunately, in the strong room, we did not install any cameras. But there are a couple of them at the entrance of the room. You can have a look' Prof. Chris offered.

He asked one of his colleagues to check the tapes. 'In the meanwhile, I want to make a list of everyone who is involved in this object you call as Chintamani'

Prof. Chris spelt the names. Mitchell asked his deputy to summon all those in the list in the next half an hour. 'I do not want to hear excuses' he said sternly.

He was very anxious to see Jenny's body. 'Can I see her body please?' he pleaded

'Sure . . . if you can handle it'

Vicky got up and the deputy took him to the cordoned off area 'Ok now. Don't touch anything. Just watch'

It was the most horrific scene he had ever seen in his life. He saw Jenny's body on the ground and her head lying beside her completely cut off and the blood had drained from her head. She was looking white as snow. The blood from her trunk had made a pool on the floor.

Vicky just turned his face and walked away. He tried to push the thoughts away. It was a trauma he found difficult to handle. No one had gotten so close in his life as Jenny. Although they never had any frank talk, the unspoken language was clear from her. She liked him and she loved him probably. If Vicky wanted to give a benefit of doubt, he cannot question their deep friendship. He realized now as he was walking with numb mind how lively and chirpy she was. She was clumsy in her ways but there was certain innocence in her.

CHAPTER: THIRTY FOUR

William Pierce started on a loud tone 'I tell you this officer because, I have been observing and learning about them for decades. The Free Masons and I suspect the Illuminati in particular must be behind this killing. They are demon worshippers and Chintamani stone held immense significance to them. I suspect that they want to give back to Lucifer what he lost in his battle with Michael'

'Professor, Whoa. We need to draw a line here. We cannot just make assumptions and malign and discredit minority religious sects' Mitchell said.

'Minority? You are gravely mistaken. Do you know that all the US President were Free Masons barring Kennedy and Nixon? Kennedy was shot and killed and people leaked on Watergate on purpose to discredit Nixon. They are immensely powerful. The bulk of American and world finances are controlled by them. They were always after the Chintamani stone. I had explained to Vicky about how Roerich claimed to have brought the Chintamani stone to the US from India or Tibet or Shambala. They lost trust in him eventually. But, you must know that the hunt had never stopped. I think we did not see foresee such a gruesome act from them'

'Although this is beside the point, how can you say that they are holding so much power in the US? If it was so, then it should have been public knowledge a long time ago. How can such things be hidden? And moreover what would they achieve by stealing the stone?'

'They along with other offshoots have been searching for an object that could make the possessor extremely powerful giving him the divinity. Let me explain it to you'

He opened his wallet and took out a One Dollar Note. He showed the reverse and asked 'What do you see?'

'A pyramid sign, then One Dollar in words and the US Seal'

'Yes. And there is more. This was designed in 1935 and President Roosevelt approved it and just changed the positioning of the Pyramid and the US Seal. Now, observe closely'. William stood up and brought the note to the center of the table.

'First please observe the Pyramid. It's a clear Masonic sign. It has an eye on it. It's the All Seeing eye. It's a sign of the Masons. The eye is that of Lucifer, the devil. Then you have the letters M-A-S-O-N placed on the star sign.

Mitchell and others leaned forward.

William continued 'Now to the seal. If you observe the larger projection of the Great Seal, you will find 13 arrows, 13 olive leaves, and 13 stripes. Please do not defend that there were initially 13 colonies. That is what they want us to believe. Coming back to the Pyramid symbol there, there are 13 steps. The US flag has 13 stripes on it.'

'We know that 13 is a cursed number that brings bad luck.'

'It doesn't end there. You must know that 13 and 6 are the numbers of the Devil'

Then he took a pen and drew lines congruently and made a six pointed star. He also did the same to the Great Seal of the US Government. It also outlined a six pointed star. Then he drew the outline of the center text which also formed a six pointed star.

'Now, look at this. There objects have been printed in the outline of six pointed stars'

'So, what is the significance?' asked William.

William took his pen again and wrote the numbers 6, 6, 6. It is 666, the number and the code of Anti-Christ.

Vicky felt uneasy with the assessment. 'Excuse me. If that is the case, then why did they have the words 'In God We Trust', the US National motto printed on it?'

'Vicky. The term God is a general term. In fact Masons prayed to their own Gods. Moreover, these words were included only in the 50s and not earlier. Just as some people started understanding the message on their currency, they printed these words to quickly defend it'

William continued 'Look at the curved lines on the right hand bottom corner. Observe closely and you will see the face of the Devil in it.' He made an outline with this pen.

'They are spread in every part of this country. Take a map of any major US city and you will find the six pointed stars on it. The initial blue print of our National Capital has been designed in such a way that it outlines shape of an Owl from the top. Owl is the symbol of Masonry. They also constructed all the major buildings in a straight line that corresponds to the rise of the Sirius star. They believe that the Sun and all the beings get the energy from Sirius, the brightest star in the sky'

Everyone listened with silence.

'Do you know why July 4th was selected as the Independence day? It's the day when the Star Sirius, the

Sun and Earth are in conjunction. You can see their signs everywhere. If you have an eye for detail, you will find that they control all the major corporations, Government, Institutions and places of worship. The Church of St. John is full of Masonic symbols. Next time, when you see the print ad for L'Oreal, you will see the pupil of the eye is in shape of an owl. CBS has the all seeing eye as its logo. Many insurance companies, stock-brokerage firms, banks have the Masonic logos. This shows their power and their presence'

'We are drifting here. What's all this has to do with the case?' Mitchell wanted to stay focused on the case.

'It's obvious. It's the work of either the Masons or the Illuminati. They have infiltrated all the sections of the Government. They do horrific acts in their Lodges and Churches and they worship Lucifer. Many believe that the stone Chintamani rightfully belongs to Lucifer and it has the power of Apotheosis—to make these people acquire super natural powers. And I do not see any other organizations who should be so much interested in this.'

CHAPTER: THIRTY FIVE

One of the deputies walked in 'Chief. Please look into this. Jennifer in the past was a victim of physical molestation and the guy who did this, Jose Soto has been released. He probably took the revenge. He probably watched her on the News and he killed her. He must have taken the stone to divert our attention.'

This was another blow to Vicky. He did not know about this side of Jenny. She looked perfectly normal to him and never showed any signs of a victim.

'Okay. Pay this rat a visit. Bring him in for questioning. I will be at the Head Quarters in less than an hour'

Mitchell continued. 'Gentlemen, we need to give a serious thought to this. No doubt. It's my job to find out who did it. But, if any of you here have anything to contribute, please feel free to contact me anytime. But, before I leave,

I want to meet each of you one-to-one to get the picture as full as possible.'

The deputy returned again 'Chief. The Feds are here. They are taking over this case.'

'What the . . .' Mitchell was upset. 'When did cases like these get into Federal Jurisdiction?' He left the room in a hurry.

William stood up 'See I told you so. I knew FBI would get involved. I am sure many in the Government will be very keen on this case.'

Vicky said 'I am not feeling too well . . .'

Prof. Chris said 'Vicky. You take a break'

'No Professor. I don't want to leave. I just need some fresh air. I will be back in a few minutes'

Akila too got up and went along with Vicky. They took a stroll out. They saw Mitchell talking to the FBI agents who in their unmistakable attire seemed to be all over the place.

'Let's get a drink Vicky' Akila said.

'You mean Soda?'

'Yes. You need some food to stay smart'

They silently sat on a bench drinking Pepsi. 'I still can't believe this is all real. If they wanted the stone, they could have just stolen it and left. Why should they kill Jenny?'

'Yes. That is what is worries everyone. I heard the Police say that she must not have felt any pain. The object used to behead was extremely sharp. I think whoever did that feared that they would be identified' Akila replied.

'You mean someone she knew?'

'It's a possibility. Or maybe someone who is easily identifiable'

'Whosoever it is Akila. They are not going to go scot free'

An hour later, Vicky was sitting in a room with FBI officer Stephen Cormack and his deputy Lisa Downing. Human mind has a funny way of anesthetizing. For a moment, Vicky was reminded of Agents Scully and Molder of X-files when he saw them.

'So, did you hand over the plank to the Police?' Stephen asked in a business-like tone.

'No. They did not ask me for it'.

'Hmm. Typical Police blunders and wonders. Where is it right now?'

'It is in my bag right here with me'

'Hand it over to us right now professor. You surely have a copy of this'

'Yes'

Stephen took a good look at the plank. He then gave it to Lisa.

'How much more time will it take for you to crack the secret of the so called mysterious stone?' Stephen asked.

'It is very difficult to put a time-line on it. I need to study the plank. I suspect the Original stone was broken down into several pieces and they were planted in all major temples across the world.'

'You must get the answers quickly professor. We want you to work with us on this case. I am assigning Agent Lisa who will co-ordinate with you on all the matters. You can forget the protocols and procedures of the University. We need to get results fast. Anything you want, I mean anything will be given to you instantly to help solve this case. No bureaucratic delays in FBI' Stephen concluded with an air of authority.

Vicky got up and he shook their hands. Lisa said that she will meet him the next day morning at Nine.

When he walked out, Akila was waiting for him. 'Vicky, Jenny was my dear and close friend. I do not want to go back to my room now. I need a real drink. You know what I mean'

'Sure Akila. Let's go some place. Then I want to get back to work pretty quickly. Now, my focus of attention is to solve this mystery and also help catch the criminal who killed Jenny.'

Vicky collected the copy of the plank and left to his room. He made a resolve not to rest until the job is done.

CHAPTER: THIRTY SIX

Vicky sent a detailed email to his parents, friends and his uncle. Such things are difficult to explain over the phone. Then he sent an email to Prof. Sastry asking his opinion on the theory that Free Masons and Illuminati were behind the killing.

As usual, Prof. Sastry replied with a theory that sounded outlandish, but had some credibility in it.

After expressing his grief over the death of Jenny, he wrote 'Vicky, Do you know that most of those who are members of these cults unwittingly engage in Tantric practices? When they go to other places such as a Masonic Lodge or a temple of Illuminati, they are in fact pursuing a path that we commonly call as 'Tantra' in India. They all pray to the wrong side of the Universal power—the power of Devil—although they do not fully understand her, unlike us who follow Hinduism in India. Almost all the

207

ancient civilizations struggled to obtain a consciousness altering experience. In order to make the brain cleanse itself from the normal thoughts and to give it a significant auto-suggestion that from that moment onwards the person would start a new life, the spiritual practitioners developed weird rituals that appear banal to horrific such as drinking blood from a skull. These practices exist in the Tantra.

Christian theology does not leave any scope for other deities to pray except perhaps to Mother Mary, the Virgin Mother. This generates positive energy and miracles happen. Some suspect that the worship of Mother Mary is the answer some of the spiritually evolved Christians found to pray to Mother Goddess. To a truly pious person, these differences fade and it is the divinity that matters.

There is similarity between Hinduism and other religions. I repeat here as I often do, that Sufism is closer to Hinduism. You are aware that Jainism and Buddhism have roots in Hinduism. The Jewish Kabala involved repetition of a word or a sound as they believe that sound has power. Some of the early Kabala practitioners took drugs and lit candles and chanted the words for hundreds of times. You can see the same practice by weak-minded sadhus in India.

So, in effect, the Masons and Illuminati are innocent and do not have any hidden agenda. They are not harmful to our society and without any reason, they along with others such as the Knights Templar or Rosicrucian's of the past were maligned without proper analysis or thought. They just happen to believe that there is much more to praying to Jesus Christ and they believe that this realization is a secret with they want to protect fearing retribution from the fundamentalist Christian organizations, who dub everything they do as evil.

Of course I too believe that some of them pray to Lucifer. Although the stone is important to them, it is not important because Lucifer once had it on his skull, but because one of the mislead member might have considered it to be the secret Talisman that would empower them to find the power to be divine. The characteristics of the stone should have given anyone a reason to carry out the stealing. But, the question is, why would they have to kill Jenny? They certainly would not want to risk the manhunt with double the efforts. Perhaps those who attend Black Mass are complete devil worshippers and they hate the Humanity. They might be behind this cruel atrocity.

You should turn your compass away from them and focus your attention on the rest of the pieces of Chintamani. As you said that there are images of other temples on the plank, they must have been hidden in these temples.

and I am sorry for having written harsh words against Jenny in the past.'

Vicky shook his head in disbelief. It's good that the Professor lives in India. If he had given lectures here like William Pierce does, someone might have shown their faith by lynching him.

As the FBI is involved in cracking the question of Jenny's death, Vicky has the job cut out for him. He must solve the mystery behind the stone. Perhaps, it will help the investigation by giving clue, as to who and why killed Jenny.

As he did not get sleep, he called Akila from his room.

'I am not able to sleep Akila'

'Well. I suggest you take some Whiskey'

'You know I don't drink alcohol.'

'You can't have sleeping pill here. That is the only alternative'

'Okay. Can you get me some Yoghurt and Rice somewhere?'

'We can try some Asian restaurant for some rice. We can get Yoghurt anywhere. I will be there in ten minutes to pick you up'

'Ok. Thanks. Good Night'

Just as he placed the receiver, there was a call from his Uncle. He was almost panicky. He saw the news. 'Vicky, I and your aunt want pick you up. Pack your bags and be ready'

'Uncle, I just can't leave. Moreover, now I am working along with the FBI to solve this case'

'Listen. Those who killed her might have you as their next target. Do you realize what kind of dangerous people you are dealing with?'

'Yes. I am fully aware and I really do not care. Those cowards got what they wanted. I am not going to let them walk free.'

'What has gotten into you? Your parents called. They were unable to get through your switch board. They are panicky. Use your calling card and talk to them.'

'Uncle, Please do now worry. I am protected and I do not fear anything. Yes. I will call them. Please take it easy'

Vicky had a very long night after getting food with Akila. Yoghurt when mixed with cooked rice has a calming effect. The lactic acid reacted with the amino acids in rice and acted as a sedative.

He spent the whole next day with Lisa explaining her, his findings.

CHAPTER: THIRTY SEVEN

In the cold basement of a New York house, a Man carefully placed an object on the table. Then he bowed down in deep respect to a framed photo. The object was Chintamani stone and the person kneeling was Lee Ho Hung and the photo was that of the 'Eternal Leader or Eternal President of DPRK, Democratic People's Republic of Korea, (better known as North Korea), King Il Sung.

Lee Hung is one of the most talented and trained spy of North Korea ever produced. Ruthless, determined and disciplined Lee helped the country to stay ahead of its arch rivals, South Korea and the United States.

A few minutes later, Lee carefully washed off all the blood stains on 'Ye Do' the traditional Korean sword. Although the traditional Korean swords were systematically hunted down and destroyed, this one was given by his father before dying. Lee vowed to take revenge and do his father proud.

213

Lee's father Chin Ho Hung was a radio operator for North Korean Army. During Korean war the allied troops were caught in a trap and Chin Hung was on the battle front everyday communicating on voice morse—an ingenious North Korean method to transmit morse code over voice channels. Lee remembered his father coming late in the night and practicing it and he also taught little Lee how to pronounce dots and dashes in a legible manner.

Lee adored his father. His father was cheerful until one day when General Mac Arthur launched an amphibian attack on Incheon and taking the North Koreans by surprise. Chin Hung was caught along with many others and he was put in a remand. Lee cried for his father.

Days went by. His mother was a school teacher. She looked very beautiful. She visited the Invading army officer's camp every day. Lee was under the impression that his mother would eventually bring his father home.

One Friday night, his mother asked Lee to stay at his Uncle's place until Monday. Lee packed his bag and left. His Uncle lived in the neighboring town. But, when he reached it, he found the house locked. Dejected, Lee returned home.

As he approached his home he heard laughter. His house was in an isolated ground and the neighboring houses were quite far away. It was dark when he returned. He could hear his Mother laughing and also a Male voice in English. His mother was an English teacher. He did not understand what they were speaking. Slowly, he went near the window and was shocked at what he saw. His mother was sitting on lap of an American Officer. He remembered the face of this officer as one day he had accompanied his mother to the camp.

She was half naked and she was mocking Lee's father. She made sounds of 'Bip Beeep Bip Bip Beeep' and both of them laughed aloud. At that age, Lee did not know much about adultery or the ways of the adults. But he was heart-broken to see his mother making fun of his father.

Lee went back to his Uncle's place and sat outside his house throughout the night. It snowed very heavily that night. But Lee was determined not to go back home without his dear father. If anyone he could trust, it was his Uncle. Next morning his Uncle and his family returned and were horrified to see little Lee frozen and running high fever. They carried him inside and nursed him. Lee broke down and asked him to help find his father. He however did not mention anything about his bad mother.

His Uncle was a local Businessman and had a large departmental store. Lee often saw the Americans visiting his stores to buy stuff. His Uncle told Lee that he could not help his father, but will try to speak to the higher officer the following day and vouch for his innocence. Next morning, he went with his Uncle who carried a big crate of Beer to the officer's camp. The senior officer was a large man with beard. His Uncle face beamed with happiness and he thanked the officer profusely. Then after a few minutes, Lee saw his father. He looked so shabby and unshaven. He hugged Lee and cried. Lee was very happy. They thanked the officer and left the place. His Uncle stayed back to talk something with the officer.

When Lee and his father returned home, it was afternoon. Lee said 'Daddy, let me bring your favorite cake and biscuits. You can go home. I will come in a few minutes'

Little Lee used his allowance money to buy his father's favorite cake and biscuits. The baker always gave Lee extra biscuits as he was very respectful. Lee ran towards his home.

Just as he entered, he heard a gunshot. The American Junior officer who was standing naked with his mother had shot his father. Chin Ho Lee fell on the floor bleeding. His mother screamed aloud and Lee dropped the package on the floor and fell and hugged his father. 'Daddy, daddy' he screamed.

His father's eyes motioned towards an object below the bed. 'Son, look at that object. Keep that with you. Learn Hwarang Do. Be loyal to our Eternal leader and our country. Do me proud' and he died.

Poor little Lee wept and he wept for days. His mother cried for a while and the junior officer went away never to be seen for a few days. Weeks later, he appeared again. His mother was now shamelessly treating him with good food and wine. He tried to be nice with Lee. But, Lee kept his silence without giving out even a single emotion 'Oh. He is just a little kid John' his mother used to say always.

When Korean war ended, the officer John Rusk and his mother got married. His mother called Lee and said that they would be leaving for the United States. Lee had no choice. That night he vowed that he would go to his enemy country and destroy it one day.

He dedicated all the time to learn English and the ways of the West. He was a brilliant student. When he reached his teenage, he asked his mother permission to visit North Korea. His mother refused. 'You are an American now Lee. They would never allow you to visit DPRK' she said. So, Lee went to South Korea. There he spent weeks to search for the master who could teach him Hwarang Do. This martial art was banned and it was secretly being taught in the deep jungles in mountainous terrain. Lee spent all his vacations to learn Korean Martial arts. He completed his engineering degree in the University of New York and was an able person. The following year, he went to South Korea and crossed the border with some of his friends. He would eventually meet with the Dear Leader, Kim Jong Il, the son of the Eternal President, who saw potential in him.

After the demise of Kim Jong Il, Lee Hung met the new leader Kim Jong-Un and a quick rapport developed between them.

CHAPTER: THIRTY EIGHT

'I am going to kick him in his ass!' President Peterson enjoyed the luxury of using foul language as gladly as President Bush Sr. once remarked openly in a press conference honoring Saddam Hussein with the same words. Now the times have changed. Saddam is dead and gone. The new enemy is the North Korean Leader Kim Jong-Un

Kim Jong-Un's father Kim Jong Il had indoctrinated the country so much that North Koreas consider him and his father as Gods, who were direct descendants from the Moon. For 23 million hungry and poor North Koreans the world was just their country and the enemies were South Korean Government and the United States not to mention the western allies.

North Korea, although isolated from the global economy fed majorly on Russia in its hue days and after Stalin had shown his indifference during the Korean war, it turned to China which in fact sent its troops in its support, when China felt its own security threatened by the allied forces. China is perhaps the only country that had influence over the regime. It is because of the Chinese, the North Korean government ran despite its foolish dictator.

Kim Jung Il was a womanizer. He has Swedish massage girls, who attend on him day and night. His private security guards were beautiful yet tough women. He fed his people less of food and more of propaganda. The people were so pathetic that they believed him fully, when he claimed that he would be sending five rockets into space to tie up the Moon and bring it to Pyongyang and put it there on a pedestal which he had constructed in shape of his own hand.

'And then I am going to pluck the US flag on it and place our flag' he roared to the cheering millions of impoverished citizens. The Television channel that night beamed the statements of the senior government officials about their plans to bring the Moon.

Every North Korean home must mandatorily have a Radio transistor and more mandatorily always keep it turned on. Surprise visits were conducted by officials to check if anyone had switched off the radio. If so, that household was in for deep trouble. The only radio channel along with the Television channel churned out utter nonsensical propaganda and hatred towards the West particularly the United States.

'Our Dear Leader did this, did that, said this, said that . . .' was the only news. Any foreigner who visited North Korea must be accompanied by a local guide given by the Government. The first place the foreigner must visit would be the shrine of Kim Il Sung, the Eternal President. There in the open court yard stands a massive statue of the dead President. Foreigners must kneel and pay respects by offering flowers.

North Korea is a paradise for those who ogle at women. The Dear leader had devised a brilliant plan to keep the frustrated male community in his country happy. He handpicked and personally selected pretty looking girls all over the country and got them trained as Traffic Police. Every junction had a pretty girl 'manning' the traffic.

Not satiated with the Swedish girls, Kim had established a system to get the best looking girls into his chamber. The local officials would go around the high schools and handpick the good looking ones. The parents of the girl 'should' feel it as their honor to send their girl as a pleasure toy to the Dear Leader. Then these girls were trained in various nuances and tastes of Kim and would eventually end up as his slaves. Those who opposed never saw the light of the day.

Kim was also known for his thirst for Hennessey VSOP Cognac which was apparently the only beverage he ever drank. He spent a cool Million Dollars every year just on the Cognac. His favorite food was Caviar. His banquets were lavish and would sometimes last for days and nights. He had girls dancing naked to please his guests. But anything and everything the 'Dear Leader' did was a miracle as he was God.

To the rest of the World, he was an enigma. He was a threat to the South Koreans who were always scared that if his regime fell, the 23 million North Koreas will infest the streets of Seoul and their economy would collapse overnight. South Koreans enjoyed the highest Standard of Living on par with the Canadians and over and above the Americans.

The high rise buildings in Seoul and other cities, the highways and their infrastructure, their discipline, their engineering standards, astonished the Americans as much as they did to the Japanese, who looked more like their lost cousins.

Now, his son Kim Jong-Un is in power. He is known to be a megalomaniac and a ruthless person. Couple of years back, he had supervised bombardment of the Yeonpyeong island with heavy artillery shells, killing 2 South Korean soldiers.

That day, Kim Jong-Un had held a meeting with his chief military officials and asked them to prepare for a new nuclear test and introduced martial law in North Korea effective from 29 January. He now had something which gave him the luxury to expend one nuclear warhead to threaten the West and also issue a direct threat to conduct pre-emptive strike against the United States and also exercise the option of launching a nuclear weapon on its soil.

The anger that took form of an expletive of doing some damage to the DPRK leader's posterior by the American President in Oval office was also promptly recorded for the next generation when the tapes would be released to the general public after a good gap of 22 years. But for the moment he cared less. He was very upset about Kim's latest act of war.

'I want to talk to the South Korean President to-night. Put it on the agenda. I also want to invite the South Korean Ambassador for dinner tomorrow here.'

'Yes Mr. President'. President Peterson has too much already on his hands. Despite having both the House and the Senate dominated by the Democrats, he had scraped through with some hard hitting pieces of legislation. America needed its medication and medication is never sweet. His popularity ratings were all time low. He was also facing allegations of not being a strong supporter of Israel, the closest and natural ally of the United States. So much so that its Prime Minister on his visit to Washington D.C had for the first time condemned the attitude of the United States as it was going soft on the Muslim terrorist outfits in the Middle East, stopping the drone attacks and closing the Guantanamo prison and sending back the inmates to respective countries. But, he is a tough President. He had the capacity to take more on his hands.

This President carried a thumb sized idol of Hanuman, the Hindu God of courage and victory always with him. He celebrated Diwali, the festival of lights in the White House. Capitol Hill also celebrated Diwali.

CHAPTER: THIRTY NINE

Lee Hung hated women. Ever since he saw his Mother acting so ignobly by marrying her husband's killer, he had lost complete trust in them. When he read Shakespeare's Hamlet, he identified himself completely with the character. He was Hamlet and his mother was Gertrude. 'Frailty, thy name is woman' was his favorite quote.

He never expressed his emotions or his anger overtly. Anger clouds one's judgment capability. It clouds one's intelligence. He has been visiting Korea for the past many years. The object which his father pointed out to him as his legacy was the 'Ye Do' sword. He learnt martial arts associated with sword fighting along with the most devastating martial art ever known to man—Hwarang Do—that can paralyze anyone in less than five seconds with just three simple moves.

When he turned 21, he devised a plan. He first joined as a salesman for an Insurance firm. Naturally, his mother and his step father were his first clientele. And what worthy clientele would they turn out to be. After all they would leave him with a wealth of ten million dollars. Less than a year, he arranged for an 'accident' He suggested that they go on a vacation to a hill station. He took the wheel taking care to wear gloves. The place was very lonely. He suddenly stopped at the edge of a deep cliff and pretended that there was some trouble with the car and he would check it out. His step father offered to help. But, Lee did not agree. He got down and carefully wiped off the steering wheel and the door handle.

Without giving a hint, he went back and then pushed the car off the steep cliff and it smashed on the ground hundreds of feet below instantly bursting into flames. A few weeks later, he collected the ten million dollars check and en-cashed it. He was now ready for bigger things in life.

He went to North Korea and underwent training under S.S.D—State Security Department, the Secret Police Department of North Korea. There he was taught all the tactics and strategies. After completion of training, he was given a rare opportunity to meet the new leader Kim Jong-Un, who was thoroughly impressed by Lee.

For a period of one year, Lee was asked to work under the US Dollar counterfeiting program. This program was curiously titled 'Room 39' by the West. Room 39 or Division 39 involved in drugs and insurance fraud in addition to counterfeiting the American Dollars. Lee did exceptionally well in his job. Later, he was sent back to the United States to engage in espionage. It was here he hit upon the idea to do away with his parents and pocket the insurance money.

That evening Lee received a call when he was in having a dinner by his private pool at home. He just finished a plate of Rice with Kimchi and Octopus. The person on the phone showed urgency of the task. The meeting that night took place in an innocuous Buddhist temple in sub urban New York. This temple was once razed to ground by some a group of ignorant people, who thought the Swastika sign on the top of the building, was a Nazi symbol. Little did they know that Swastika and Om are the symbols of Hinduism and Swastika was used by Hitler to claim Aryan superiority. Swastika is also used by the Korean Buddhists to put on their temples. The new version of the building is a shadow of its former structure.

The person who met Lee was an octogenarian working for the S.S.D. He greeted him in a very soft voice. 'Annyeong Haseyo' literally meaning 'Are you at Peace?'. The Koreans are mostly peace loving, Korea itself being 'The Land of the Morning Calm'. On the contrary, this conversation was between two people who loving anything far from Peace.

'Pyongyang wanted you to take up this task and exercise all means necessary to get the Chintamani stone from

227

Rixton University. You will use this ID card as a press reporter and you are going to visit Rixton tomorrow and seek invitation for the Press meet. This will give you enough opportunity to assess the security systems and device a plan.'

S.S.D has come of age. It now has network in as many as sixty countries globally. Its agents are often martial art experts with special weapons training. They are deployed as embassy officials or they are stationed in various countries posing as students. It is funded by Room 39 which had amassed billions of dollars out of its illegal businesses. Its agents are ruthless and inhuman. They are trained to survive without food and water for long periods of time.

Next morning, Lee called the University and went on to meet with Jenny. She explained about the discovery and also registered Lee's details for the Press meet. The following day, Lee attended the Press meet. Jenny was the person who was in charge of the stone and the plank and he knew that she alone can bring it out to him. Lee stayed back that day. All the Press reporters had left. He went to Jenny's office and requested her for additional close up photos of the Stone. She readily obliged. Lee took the photographs and left the place.

On Monday morning, Jenny received a call. It was Lee. He sounded panicky. 'Ms. Jennifer, I have forgotten my bag in your office and now I realize that my digital camera is also inside. It also contains very important photographs.

I have to leave for Seoul on an urgent work and my flight is this Noon. Can you please do me a favor? I am already in the University Campus. Can you please come down and open the keys. It won't take more than a minute'

Security was lax in the early hours. The snow was cruel and there was no one in sight. Lee had enough time to go around the building and snap off the surveillance camera cables.

As Jenny walked towards the building, she pitied the guy. He had the charm of a college student. He was bright and said that his favorite sport was rowing. A few minutes later, she found Lee with a backpack containing a long barrel shaped content on his back. 'What's that?' she asked.

'Oh. That is my rowing equipment' Lee smiled.

Once they were inside, Lee pretended to search. Then he said 'I think I left it inside the locker room where the stone is kept.'

'That's impossible. That area is checked doubly before it is locked'

'Please Ms. Jennifer. It would not take a minute. Please open and glance inside once. I will wait here.'

Jenny made the most horrible mistake of her life. She opened the locker room and she glanced inside. And then she turned back. Lee had just opened his backpack and revealed the long sword. Even before she understood what was happening, in a quick flash he severed her head from her body. Blood gushed out of her trunk and her body fell on the ground. Without wasting any time, Lee jumped into the room. He broke the glass case and stole the Stone. He searched for the plank. He could not find it. He disappeared into the snowy parking lot.

CHAPTER: FORTY

'Vicky. You got it all wrong. FBI does not investigate super natural phenomena. We do not have any X-files department. You seem to watch X-files a lot. When people see an UFO or if cattle or corn fields are mutilated, the general public informs us. We get all kinds of reports. We just file them. We do not investigate them. People have attributed many stories to our agency. They think that we have stolen the documents from Nikola Tesla when he died in 1943. Nikola Tesla was a renowned Physicist. He was the one who explained the phenomenon of alternating current and people think that he had discovered the way to make the dangerous 'Particle Beam' or what has been popularly called as the 'Death Ray'. We are also accused of not co-operating with other agencies. But all of this is untrue'

'Then why are you investigating the missing Chintamani?'

'Good question. It is for many reasons. First, we are answerable to the Mexican Government. It is their property. Second, we have a strong reason to believe that a dangerous cult is behind this. Third, it is a matter of protecting human heritage. The stone is a mysterious discovery in the jungles of Mexico.' Lisa did not want to reveal the fact that the order had come from the highest ranks of her agency, the Director's office.

'So, Is there any progress on the investigation?' asked Vicky.

'Yes. We have made some headway. Jose is not involved. Apparently, there was a person of Asian origin involved in this. We checked through all the people who had attended the Press meet. Only one particular reporter had shown keen interest on this subject. His name on the records is Lee Dixon. He had shown the documents as working for a Korean newspaper'

'He had cut off all the surveillance cameras with a sharp object. We believe that he used a Sword to behead her. Based on the Tissue Trauma, Forensics and Medical team concluded that it's a sword particularly of traditional type. By the time the surveillance room got the hang of it, it was too late.

'I want to have a look at the suspect's photograph. Can you show me?'

'Yes. I will do that later. But, I also want to tell you that we are focused on the theory that an Asian cult is involved in this crime. Your analysis only points out that there could be many more pieces of the Chintamani stone in Asia. As you are the only expert on this subject, I have been asked by my superiors to fly with you to these places and solve the puzzle'

'Chintamani stone has the ability to transform a person into a Super human. It can make people invincible. Yes. There might have been these pieces of stone long back at these places. But, I do not think you will find any of the stones there now'

'Simple logic, all these temples are dysfunctional. No one goes there to pray. So, the last of the priests and public who knew about the stone would have surely taken it away as they had taken away all the ornaments and gold from these temples' Vicky replied.

'But what if the later generations were not aware of the stone that was hidden somewhere? When you can find it in Mexican temple, why not in Asia then'

'I have already spoken with the CIA office. I have scheduled a briefing with them this evening.'

'Should I attend as well Lisa?'

'No. You are not authorized'

With the Indian Passport, he could visit only Thailand, Sri Lanka, Hong Kong and Nepal without any prior visa. If he has to travel to Indonesia or other countries, he needed visa stamping at those specific country consulate offices.

Lisa on the other hand did not have any such problems. There are 300 Countries and Territories in the World. An American can travel 160 Countries and Territories without any prior visa. An American obtains a visa after he/she lands in that country.

But as FBI is involved in this case, Vicky had an assurance that he will get all the visas without any delay. He had to visit Cambodia, Thailand, Indonesia and India. There was no reason to visit Mexico as the stone had been retrieved from that country. As the American government is involved the visas would be obtain in a couple of days which otherwise would have taken weeks to obtain.

CHAPTER: FORTY ONE

Vicky badly wanted a change of scene. He got on to NJ Transit and went to Central Park. He wanted to spend time alone. He sat below a tree and tried to connect the pieces.

'Why was the stone stolen? Perhaps it will be sold in the black market for a high price. Perhaps it was most sought after by some occult cult. Perhaps it has been the eternal quest of some secret societies.'

His phone buzzed. 'Vicky?'

'Yes Lisa'

'Where are you?'

'I am at the Central Park.'

235

'Now you listen carefully. Get out of that place right now and hop into a Taxi and go the NYPD Head Quarters and stay put. Call me when you reach there. Your life is in danger. Do not, I repeat do not stop or talk to anyone' I am getting you a back-up. But, under the circumstances, this is the best possible option. It takes you less than half an hour to reach."

'Okay Got it.' Vicky got up and walked towards the exit. At a distance he spotted two Asian men walking towards him hurriedly. And then he saw the third person walking a few paces behind them. He looked familiar. He was Professor Dietrich.

He increased the pace and did not look back. On the street he spotted a cab. He avoided it and walked past the sidewalk in the opposite direction. At the traffic signal he spotted another cab. In a flash he jumped into it and asked the cab to take him to One Police Plaza. He then sulked into the seat so as to appear invisible from outside. The car stopped with a screech. He heard doors banging. Instinctively, he crawled to the other door and started running. He heard someone shouting 'Vicky, Stop.' Then he heard the gunshots. He ran across the main road as he had no choice. Another gunshot and this one scraped by his shoulder.

Vicky then spotted NYPD cars with blazing lights coming in his direction. His quick mind told him that he stood more chances of surviving if he just fell down on the sidewalk. As he fell the third bullet just whisked past him.

NYPD cars halted with a screech beside him and the cops took out their assault weapons. They could not identify the shooter. They radioed for an ambulance. Vicky was bleeding.

The second bullet scraped through his shoulder and ripped his shirt off. Immediate first aid was given by the cops. He remained calm. The ambulance was there in matter of seconds and he was bandaged by the medics.

Lisa arrived at NYPD Head Quarters. Vicky briefed her on what transpired. She immediately made a call and talked about possible involvement of Dietrich. Just as she snapped the phone, a detective entered the cabin.

'Lisa, we had a man shot dead near the place where we picked up Vicky. He looks familiar. We ran his profile and we identified him as Professor Dietrich'

'There is some connection then. Vicky, I want you to relax here. I will drive you to the campuses. Lisa walked out.

After a while she returned 'Okay listen. You can't go back to the Campus. You need protection and you are a sitting duck if you go back. We have identified a safe house. You will stay there. We will arrange to get your stuff.'

'Okay Lisa. Whatever you say'

'And one more thing, give me your cellphone. You are not going to use this anymore. We will give you a non-traceable super cellphone. You can call your family and tell them you are safe. I just got some Intel which I can't share with you. All I can say is that the stone is in the wrong hands and those guys are planning to use it in Nuclear weapons program. Couple of officials from the Department of Defense, are eager to meet you. You will see them tomorrow.'

CHAPTER: FORTY TWO

Things were getting surreal for Vicky. Suddenly, life got on to a feverish pace. It emerged later that Dietrich was a member of some fringe Neo Nazi organization that was Anti-Semitic and Anti-American. He was in touch with North Korean S.S.D and he was killed by the North Koreans.

CCTV footage ran the North Korean attackers faces and they were identified as two students. They had left their apartment.

Next day the DoD officials discussed at length about Chintamani. The atmosphere was somber. North Korea or D.P.R.K has witnessed sudden increased activity at the highest levels of the Government.

The officials were keen to know if there was any way the power of the Stone could be neutralized. Vicky said that

239

theoretically speaking the stone was just a fragment of a larger stone and according to his theory all the pieces are energetically interconnected. They had organic characteristics of life force and energy.

Vicky had called his family and lied to them that he was going on a long drive to various Universities around the United States and that he would be calling them whenever possible.

That evening while having dinner, he was shocked to learn that the two Korean students had committed suicide by shooting themselves. S.S.D operates on cult-like lines. The operatives are indoctrinated at a very young age. Failure of mission is considered a disgrace and punishable by death. They draw heavily from the Samurai of Japan who used to commit hara-kiri if they fell short of the expectations.

Such ruthlessness makes the S.S.D a very persuasive and dangerous organization. Vicky now is on the hit-list of its American division. His survival now is now increasingly getting correlated to the success of his mission. But, the trouble was that he did not what his mission was.

Lisa brought him a fake beard and hair color. She asked him to put it on and said that she will have to take a few photographs. Vicky obliged without asking any questions. Next day she gave him an American passport with his new disguise photo and a nationality neutral name, Samuel Johnson.

Vicky discussed the itinerary with her. The objective now was to find out the secret at least as shown on the plank. If any connection could be established amongst these pieces of stones, it would help him to understand the power of the stolen Chintamani.

His wound started healing rapidly. The muscle tear was painful Vicky realized how fortunate he was to be alive. He knew that death does not end a person completely. A part of the consciousness remains and that is considered as soul or the spirit. But, without the physical body nothing much can be accomplished.

He made a phone call to Unni Krishnan, his mentor in Kerala, who had advised Vicky to being the chant of Rudra Jaap. When Rudra Abhishekam or the holy consecration of Shiva is not possible or when Rudra Homam or the holy fire sacrifice to Shiva is not possible, reciting the verses of this powerful text gives equal benefits. His mentor had advised him to recite one particular line which he explained as the heart of all the sacred texts.

There are four Vedas or Books of Knowledge in Hinduism. Out of them three are the key religious texts. The middle one is called Yajur Veda that deals with the rituals and hymns of prayer. In that text the center most verse is that of Rudra Dhyaayam. And at the center of this lies that single line which is the most favorite of God Shiva 'Om Namo Bhagavate Rudraaya'. This imbibes divine strength and power to the reciter.

CHAPTER: FORTY THREE

Lisa and Vicky had to fly Emirates up to Dubai where they had to change the flight to Thai Airways to Bangkok. After a non-eventful flight to Dubai, they relaxed at the Airport after consuming complimentary breakfast. A couple of hours later, they boarded the flight and occupied the two seat window row on Thai Airways Dubai to Bangkok Non-Stop. The first country they planned to visit was Thailand.

The flight stewardess politely folded her hands and said 'Sawasdee ka' Vicky felt at home instantly. This gesture of folding hands as a mark of respect originated in India. Air India's stewardesses had perfected the art of 'Namaste' followed by the Sri Lankan's air hostesses and the Thai.

'I think there are many similarities between India and Thailand.' Lisa asked.

'Yes. There are. What strikes me the most is their National Emblem. It's Garuda, the giant Eagle that is the vehicle of God Vishnu. Did you see the name of the Airport in Bangkok on your boarding card? It is Suvarnabumi International Airport. Suvarnabumi was the name given to the geographical regions eastern and south eastern side of India by the ancient Hindus. Thailand was ruled by Hindu Monarchs and the Thais were Hindus until the Buddhists destroyed the religion and converted most of the Hindus. Yet, there are many aspects of Hinduism that still exist in Thailand. I have read that much. I need to explore more when we reach there'

'It is quite fascinating.'

'Yes. Can you please give me 5 minutes? I want to quickly go through my prayer.' Vicky pulled out a Business card holder from his shirt pocket.

'This was my mobile temple. It has all the images of the deities I used to pray to'

'Can I have a look?' Lisa was curious

'Sure' He gave it to her

Starting with the image of Ganesh or Ganapati, the folder had small card size images of various Hindu Gods. Then towards the end, Lisa was surprised to find the image of Jesus Christ and then the Kaaba.

'So, do you pray to Jesus and Allah?' she asked.

'Yes. I do Lisa'

'How can you do that? Is there no restriction in your religion?'

'No. There is not. Moreover, all the religion preach Universal Truth and all the religions have the same basic rituals and beliefs. For instance, the Christians and Moslems have Holy water. So do the Hindus. The Christians have their own theory of Trinity. Hindus also have that. Some Christians believe in baptizing. Hindu priests follow this practice. Christians sing hymns. Hindus sing Bhajans.'

'But I am sure there are lot of differences between Hinduism and Islam'

'No Lisa. We have many similarities. The Hindus revolve around the sanctum sanctorum to cleanse their bad karma. It is important to note that the circumbulations are done in clockwise direction. So, do the millions of Haj pilgrims who visit Mecca. They go around the Kaaba seven times. The Hindus believe in sacred water. There is a sacred fountain near Kaaba. The Hindus wear two pieces of white cloth when they go to important temples to perform important religious worship. So, do the Haj pilgrims wear two pieces of white cloth and nothing else when they go to Mecca.'

'Oh my God'

'There is more Lisa. The word 'Kaaba' itself I learnt recently originated from the word 'Kaapaali' which is one of the names of Lord Shiva. Likewise, Hindus also worship the name 'Allah'. It is one of the names we chant when we pray to our Mother Goddess'

'Look at this Lisa.' Vicky pointed out to the corner of the picture with Arabic text.

'Do you know what it is?' he asked

'No. Not the faintest idea'

'This is 786 in Arabic text. They consider this as the holiest symbols. 'Now, come with me to the bathroom'

'Whoa. What?'

'Just come with me. You have not put on your seat belts yet'. Vicky pulled her hand and took her to the lavatory and opened the door. He and she were facing the mirror.

'Now, what do you see?' He pointed out the card on the mirror

'I don't know. I had seen it somewhere though'

'Yes. You have seen it here in one of my Hindu God's photos. It's the symbol of Om. You reverse it and this is what you get 786'

'Now let's get back to our seats. There is more. Are you ready?'

'Yeah, Go ahead'

'Devout Muslims have been visiting Mecca since the days of the Prophet. Some original articles of worship were from India. One vessel in Mecca is said to have been brought from India. It had inscriptions written by King Vikramaditya of India. Of course, Vikramaditya and his kingdom were long gone when this took place. But the vessel must be something special and sacred to have been sent to Mecca.'

'Do you have proofs of all this Vicky?'

'Yes. This area was part of Hindu kingdom once upon a time. All this is written in a book called 'Sayar-ul-Okul'. I read that this is specified on Page 315 of this book. The original volume still exists in the Makhtab-e-Sultania Library in Istanbul. Turkey.

'The human instinct is similar no matter what the religion.'

'Yes. There are many. For instance, during the holy month of Ramadan or Ramzan or Lebaran, the Muslims go on a fast based on the Lunar position. Hindus do the same. We call it as 'Chandrayan Vrat'. In some Indian mosques, burnt sandal ashes are given as a holy object. You will find the same practice in Hindu temples. In fact some Dargahs in India named after some Sufi saints are visited by the Hindus in large numbers. There is one such Dargah in Ajmer dedicated to Khwaja Moinuddin Chisti. We call it as 'Gareeb Nawaz'. Emperor Akbar was said to have visited it by walking on foot to fulfill his vow after his wife gave birth to a Son. Many Indians visit it. In fact, I want to visit this holy shrine someday.'

'Then why do you guys fight a lot?'

'All of us do not fight. There are extremists in every religion. There are extremists in Hinduism, Buddhism, Jainism, and Christianity and also in Islam. All religions teach peace. Islam is perhaps the most misunderstood religion in the world. Prophet Mohammad had asked his followers to protect the weak and the good. He mentioned the Jihad or the Holy war not against other innocent humans, but against injustice and evil forces. Unfortunately, as it happened in every religion, including Hinduism, some vested interests mislead the followers by giving their own interpretations to it. If you want to learn more about Islam, you must observe the life of a pious Muslim'

'I am impressed Vicky. It's been a lively conversation'

'Yes. It's going to be a long flight'

CHAPTER: FORTY FOUR

'Bangkok' or as it is earlier known 'Krung Thep' is the shorter version of the longest name of a city in the world. Its original name is 'Krung Thep Mahanakhon Amon Rattanakosin Mahinthara Yuthaya Mahadilok Phop Noppharat Ratchathani Burirom Udomratchaniwet Mahasathan Amon Piman Awatan Sathit Sakkathattiya Witsanukam Prasit'

Bangkok has two faces. One, that is spiritual, soft and the other wild, dangerous with colorful nightlife. Bangkok has been sinking 2 inches every year and it perhaps the hottest city on the planet.

The plane landed in the luxuriant Suvarnabumi International Airport. There was a chubby American with a colorful shirt and sunglasses, holding a placard with for Lisa's name on it. He quietly escorted them out of the airport into a BMW MPV Truck.

Vicky always dreamt of racing such a car. The Americans loved European and Japanese cars. Only a few who owned a BMW understood that the letters stood for Bathlomew Motoren Werks or Bavarian Motor Works. Lesser number knew that the BMW logo signifies rotating blades of a plane, because BMW was initially intended to make Airplane engines and not cars.

As is the case with all modern International airports, this one too was constructed way outside the Bangkok city. The drive ways were impressive.

'Is this your first time in Bangkok Lisa?'

'Yeah John, Why are the cabs in Candy colors here?'

'Bangkok is a colorful city. Each color represents a Taxi company here. The cabs are efficient. As you can see most of them are Toyota Corollas'

'Oh. I see' The driveway to the city was impressive and clean.

Vicky wondered when he might see his city Chennai like that. 'Not in my generation' he thought.

'Okay. Listen up. I am gonna put you guys in Grand Hyatt. It's a great place. Then we are going to spend some time on the streets exploring the culture. Tomorrow early morning, we will drive down the Ayuthya.'

'Thanks John. So, what are the street specialties?'

'Whoa. Almost everything, The food is Great. They serve everything with Jasmine rice. It is awesome. If you are adventurous, you can try Fried Cockroaches or Fried Caterpillar tonight'.

'Oh come on' said Lisa

'I am not kidding Lisa. You get this stuff'

'Okay John. Point taken'

'Alright, now, go through this. This is the update we have on what you are looking for' John handed over a packet to Lisa.

It contained a brief report on Ayuthya. Ayuthya was a kingdom that flourished in Thailand in the 12th Century. It has many Hindu temples. The photograph of one of the Temple was enclosed.

'Take a look at this' Lisa showed it to Vicky.

'Yes. This is where we have to go'

'Good. So, you guys are well prepared. Looks like your two guys have their gear ready' Lisa seemed happy.

Vicky asked out of curiosity. 'Who is coming along with us?'

John replied 'They are engineers Vicky. They are coming along with stone penetrating vision equipment. They will help us detect any of the hidden treasures or stones. It cuts our chase'

'I am impressed John. How did you get this technology' asked Vicky.

'It is one of the babies of CIA. They won't tell us much Vicky. But that's CIA for you. Right John?' teased Lisa.

'Yeah, You Feds enjoy your home and the excitement. We end up eating fried cockroaches' It was a light moment.

'So you guys want to hear a story?' continued John.

'Sure. Go Ahead'

'It's about the hotel I am taking you now—Grand Hyatt. There was another Hotel in its place which was demolished in 1987. It was called the Erawan Hotel, owned by the Government. When this hotel was being constructed in 1956, there were series of accidents and delays. The shipload of Italian Marble went missing. Then a Hindu priest advised the Government to sanctify the place by constructing a temple by the side of the site. He said that the place had lot of negative energy as it was once up a time used to stone and to punish the criminals by the public. Once the temple Erawan was constructed, the bad things stopped. Now, the place looks excellent and many tourists visit the temple. There are many Hindu Gods in that temple. I can't spell the names. Vicky. You might want to check that out. It's just adjacent to the Hotel'

'Thanks John. It's quite interesting. I am eager to see'

After checking in, John informed them that he would be back by seven. Vicky had three hours. He quickly took a shower and then went walking to the temple.

The temple Erawan, he realized was named after 'Irawat' the elephant vehicle of Indra, the King of Gods. The temple had a multistoried structure and the roof had the three headed elephant. Vicky went inside. He was astonished to see Indra idol kept at the first level. In fact, it was Indra who was propitiated along with the fire God, Agni in the Vedas. In the basement, there was a Museum with many statues of all Hindu Gods and the places where they are brought from. They were from all parts of Thailand and bordering Cambodia.

In the compound, he saw the idol of Brahma, who the Hindus stopped praying to. The priest there told Vicky that the earlier statue was vandalized by a lunatic and that lunatic was killed by the bystanders. Vicky went up the stairs and on the top most floors, he saw the statue of Buddha. Devotees knelt down and meditated. Vicky found immense peace of mind at that place.

He understood how the Thais had synthesized the Hindu Gods with Buddhism. He walked back to his room and ordered food. Then reading through the tourist attractions, he fell asleep.

That night, he spent time with John and Lisa who were very cheerful. They visited the streets of Bangkok. They ate at a traditional Thai restaurant.

When they drove around, Vicky saw a massive statue of Lord Ganesa outside the Bangkok World Trade Center.

When Vicky wanted to do a bit of shopping, he was accosted by a pimp who was keen on getting Vicky's attention for the services of massage and others. Vicky lost his mood for shopping and headed back to John. He felt bad how a good country spoilt its reputation this way. He wanted to go back to the Hotel. Next day morning, he has to get his act right.

CHAPTER: FORTY FIVE

After the standard buffet breakfast at the Coffee shop, they started their journey. Their destination is an ancient city by name Ayuthya. This ancient city named after 'Ayodhya' of India, now lay in ruins. It is situated 50 miles from Bangkok.

Ayuthya was also knows as Siam. The city was built in 1350 by King Ramathibodi. He was ruling the neighboring Lop Buri. However as smallpox and other epidemics infested his Capital, he built Ayuthya dedicated to Lord Rama of Ayuthya. He constructed the city surrounded by canals. It was called as Venice of East. In its zenith of glory, this city was the largest in the world.

King Ramathibodi, as was the practice of all Thai kings, followed both Buddhism and Hinduism. He proclaimed himself as the incarnation of Lord Vishnu. It was suspected that a Sage had given him some secret

255

object. From that day onwards, the King had become very powerful. Ramathibodi conquered the neighboring kingdoms. He made all the kings in the region as his Vassals and followed the Mandala system, giving them autonomy yet had federal control.

After generations, the Kingdom lost its Glory. There were repeated attacks from Burma and in 1767 the city was destroyed.

Two new people joined the group. They were Burmese by origin but to Vicky's surprise, both were Hindus. Their specialization was imaging and they had with them the most advanced equipment—infra red cameras that can see objects through one inch thick wall.

'You guys are not going to tamper anything other than the stone that is if and when you find it. The site is now proclaimed as Ayutthaya historical park, and it is now known internationally as a UNESCO World Heritage site. You can expect guards there. So, if you have to take the stone, you have to steal it. It was very difficult for me to convince the authorities that our intentions were noble' John warned the engineers.

Vicky sat along with them on the last row. 'But, why do we have to steal it? I don't understand'

'Vicky. You gotta wake up man. Thailand would never let go of such an important object of mystical and religious value. It will be considered as a part of their Heritage and will end up in the Royal Museum. I don't get my paycheck from the Thai Government. I get it from the United States to which I owe allegiance'

Vicky stretched back to strike a conversation with the engineers.' So, how did you come to Thailand?'

'Our family escaped the military junta of Burma and fled to Cambodia. Then we had to flee from Khmer Rouge.'

'I am Vicky'

'I am Rambhupal and my brother is Rosanbhupal'

'Once upon a time, Myanmar was a part of India. Our ships used to head straight out east and land at your seaports. Many of our families had settled in your country' said Vicky.

'But then, there are so many cultural differences. We have lost our roots. But, we still held on to our religion. Do you know that once upon a time, our country was called Ramanna Desa and all the kings had the names Rama?'

'Burma or Myanmar's first name was 'Indra Dwipa' and your country was famous for its tin mines. After the Hindu Kings sought to establish the 'Rama Rajya' the utopian kingdom of justice, prosperity, peace and wellness they changed the name to 'Ramanna Desa'. After their decline, the country was renamed as 'Myanma' or 'Myanmar'. Later, the resurgence of culture occurred and the name changed to 'Brahma Desa' which got corrupted as 'Burma Desa' or simply 'Burma'.

'Wow. You know more about our country that we do'

'No. These are certain things that I had read about. I am aghast that in spite of all these countries showing urge to show their Hindu roots, it is only a few countries such as Burma who try to wipe out the roots?

'Yes. That is why we left our country'

'We usually do a study of the place where we are asked to do our work.'

'Interesting, Can you please tell me about this place we are going? I just saw an outline of the temple.' asked Vicky.

'Okay. The place where we are going is Ayuthya, and the temple we are going to do our research is called 'Wat Phra Ram' or 'The Temple of King Ram'. This temple was built by Ramesuan, the son of Ramathibodi, over the site where King Ramathibodi was cremated. However, the temple was not built fully until 100 years. You will find the Hindu images of Garuda and Naga on it.'

'It is strange. We have seen the images of Garuda and Nagas on the temple of Chichen Itza in Mexico as well' Vicky was trying to establish a connection between these two civilizations.

It was a bright day. When they reached the site, it looked intriguing.

'Such a place of immense heritage and yet not a soul in sight.' Vicky remarked.

'Yeah, That makes our job easier' John wanted to get this done as quickly as possible.

'Okay. We will start our work. We will beam our cameras on places you ask us' said Ramabhupal.

There was a pond by the side of the temple with fully blossomed lotus flowers. Vicky took a few moments to breathe in and focus.

Then they started the work. Wall by wall, they scanned. They scanned the inner parts of the Sanctum. There were idols of Rama inside. Vicky was disappointed.

As they walked, it occurred to Vicky that they must go to the spot where the king might have been cremated. This required the infra red cameras to be trained on the ground.

Lisa whispered. 'But why would such a stone get cremated along with the king's body? Would it not be considered powerful enough for his successors to hold on to?'

'Perhaps, the King did not get a chance to tell his Son. His death might have been sudden and unexpected'

'Good reason'. Then the camera caught an object showing brilliant luster below the ground.

The Burmese brothers set out to dig the ground. Suddenly both of them started to puff and pant. 'I can't breathe, oh my God, I can't breathe' screamed the elder one and he ran away from the spot. His younger brother followed him. They could finally catch the wind and breathed heavily. Vicky was reminded of what Professor Ramos underwent in his attempt to get the stone.

Vicky reached for the shovel and with prayer on his mind started digging the place. A sudden gust of wind blew up the find sand blinding everyone. But, Vicky continued chanting louder and then the gust disappeared. Everything became silent after a violent shake of the ground.

Chintamani had the power to protect itself. Once the defensive shield is overcome, it surrenders to the holder. Now, the brothers joined Vicky and after half an hour they sighted the stone. Vicky bent forward and grabbed it.

In the meantime, John had taken the guards and offered them Marlboro cigarettes and chit chat. The soil surrounding the stone had melted Gold chunks. Vicky put them into the cover and quickly put it in the bag. They filled back the soil and walked towards the truck. John saw the team getting into the vehicle and he hopped in after bidding the guards farewell.

In the truck, Vicky was very excited. He felt the same energy from the stone as he did when he held the Chintamani stone taken from Mexico.

'Yes. We did it Lisa'

'Good job. But did you get any clues to crack the puzzle?'

'No. But I collected the melted Gold nuggets. Surprisingly, this stone has the same size and shape of the missing one.'

'I am feeling like the King of the world. This is very powerful. It did not burn along with the body' Vicky held it in his hands.

'Are we leaving for Cambodia tonight' asked Vicky after a while.

'No. That is scheduled for tomorrow morning. I need to send a brief to my Boss' Lisa left.

Vicky spent rest of the evening watching 'Ramakian' the Thai version of the Indian Hindu epic 'Ramayan'. He had heard about this as a student. But, he was thrilled to see how every part of Thai tradition was touched by Hinduism.

Later, he compared the images of Nagas and Garuda of Wat Prah Ram and Chichen Itza of Mexico. There was a strong connection between this civilization.

Packing the Chintamani stone and concealing it from the Airport scanners was a challenge. Suvarnabumi International Airport had the state of the art equipment and this stone can easily be confiscated by the authorities. Vicky was concerned.

'Don't worry about it Vicky. Let me show you something' Lisa went to her room and carried a small black box

'What's that?'

'It's a special box made out of HSNC or High Spectrum Nano Carbon that will show it only as a small black box to the scanner'

No wonder billions are spent on Research & Development activities to support these agencies.

CHAPTER: FORTY SIX

Cambodia or 'Kambuja' as it was known in ancient time, was believed to have derived its name from the Sage Kamban who hailed from South India. This kingdom reached its peak of glory under Suryavarman II. His forefathers migrated from the island of Java or Yawa. King Siva Varman, who had destroyed the ancient Mayans who attacked his kingdom by cleverly using Hobbits, 20,000 years earlier, was one of his ancestors.

King Suryavarman also believed that he was incarnation of God Vishnu. Vicky noted this similarity of Apotheosis between King Ramathibodi of Ayuthya and Suryavarman of Kambuja. Both believed that they were incarnations of God Vishnu. If the former had a piece of Chintamani, then there is a high probability that the latter to would also have had. This begs a question. 'Does Chintamani stone makes the person believe that he was divine?'

As Vicky and others entered the departure lounge of Suvarnabumi airport, they were awe-struck by a gigantic colorful statue depicting the Churning of the Milky Ocean by the Gods and Demons of Hindus. The characteristics and the art were typically Indian in origin. It spread the entire width of the main lobby of the departure lounge. It was so massive that it took Vicky ten minutes to just observe the details.

He also found paintings and pictures of Thai royalty. The Thai Royal family followed the Hindu practices and worship. The coronation ceremony was dominated by Hindu rituals. The so called 'Cuda karma' of Thai royal youth was that of Hindu. When the Thai royalty died, they are cremated in the Hindu method. Every king was addressed as 'Rama' in Thailand.

The flight to Siem Reap was a short one. The name 'Siem Reap' meant 'Defeat of the Siem' (or Thailand). This city was closest to Angkor Wat Temple which was less than an hour drive. This temple is the next destination for Vicky. The significance of this temple dedicated to God Vishnu, is so great for Cambodia that they had placed the outline of this temple on their National flag.

John, who had visited almost all the cities in the region, was upbeat about Siem Reap.

'Vicky' he remarked 'You want to see Apsaras dancing?'

'How do you know about Apsaras?' Vicky reacted.

'Who are Apsaras?' asked Lisa

'Apsaras are divine nymphs who danced in the Heaven in the court of God Indra'

'So, how come there are in Cambodia?'

John explained 'The girls give a great performance in the City market area. They dance like Apsaras'

'John. You seem to have a pretty good time in Asia' Lisa laughed.

'It's part of my job, lady. We are going to stay in a very beautiful hotel. It's called 'Grand Hotel d'Angkor'. It's a 90 year old building and was the favorite choice of the likes of Charlie Chaplin and Jackie Kennedy.

'Wow' Vicky was spell bounded when he looked at the lush green frontage of the Hotel.

'Tomorrow is a big day. Let's meet up and go out tonight'

Vicky was least interested in sightseeing. But, he did not want to play spoilsport. So, he accompanied the Burmese brothers, Lisa and John to the market. He observed many traditions of Cambodians resembling those of Hindus.

'I don't want to be adventurous tonight. I want KFC' Vicky asked.

'Sure. Let's go to KFC' John said.

Next morning, they set out to Angkor Wat. All of them were aware that Angkor Wat was the Largest Temple complex in the world. So, if they are lucky, they could find what they wanted in a day or two.

When they reached the place, Vicky gasped for breath looking at the sheer dimension of the temple. It was colossal. The temple was surrounded by a moat with huge width. The Causeway that leads to the temple was flanked by a balustrade of Naga or Serpent statues, each of which was towering over 70 feet.

Walking through the passage made Vicky's knees go weak. This complex was named 'Vrah Vishnulok' or 'Vira Vishnulok', the 'Grand World of Lord Vishnu' and it is spread around in miles.

The majestic grandeur of this temple cannot be described in writing. 'Angkor' originated from the word 'Nogor' or 'Nagar' which meant a 'City' and 'Wat' originated from the Sanskrit word 'Vatika' or a 'Shrine'. So 'Angkor Wat' meant 'The Shrine City'

The complex had many shrines each one dedicates to a Hindu God. The main temple had the statue of Lord Vishnu. Someone had placed a few flowers in front of the idol. The place was serene.

Common sense suggested that they train the Infra red camera in the main temple. And so they stared there. Unfortunately, they could not detect anything interesting. They moved from one wall to another, one temple to another. However, by evening, they had drawn blank.

They had decided to return the following day.

CHAPTER; FORTY SEVEN

There were dozens of small shrines that were empty devoid of the divine idols. Most of them were destroyed by the invading armies. After the death of Suryavarman, the kingdom declined and so did the temple.

The most horrible part of Cambodia's history was the rule of Khmer Rouge under Pol Pot between 1975 and 1979. As the French had ruled for about 90 years, this country has lot of French culture and language. The word 'Rouge' being 'Red', Khmer Rouge was a communist organization that tried social engineering driving everyone from the doctors to engineers to plough the fields.

Khmer Rouge soldiers would line up a family headed by a professional either a Doctor or an Engineer or a Businessman and send each one of them to various work camps so, dividing them forever.

269

More than four millions have died under their rule. There were death camps and anyone who resisted or opposed were sent to these killing fields.

Khmer Rouge destroyed most of the ancient cultures. They completely erased the cultural and traditional legacy of Cambodia. They could not destroy Angkor Wat, as it would have taken them considerable resources for the project. In spite of it, some damage was done by the miscreants and also the over-enthusiastic US Air Force who dropped couple of bombs over it, as they suspected that enemies were hiding inside, the temple remained albeit in ruins. The restoration program still continues.

In the evening next day, it occurred to Vicky that if such kings were obsessed with Chintamani, then they might have been cremated along with it or they might have set it in their own statue. Vicky led the team to carefully check every idol thrown around in the courtyard. Some of the statues did not have heads. Some lost their hands and feet.

One of the idols, resembled that of God Vishnu but without his usual features, apparently a depiction of King Suryavarman. It had a pedestal stone base and it looked as though it was set on the pedestal. The infra red camera depicted the stone at the base of the pedestal. The statue was too heavy to lift. Vicky did not want to break the statue. They had to somehow cut the base and remove the stone.

They went back to the Hotel.

'There are two ways to go about it. Either inform the Government and let the news out or to steal it as we had done in Thailand.' Lisa said.

'Whoa. I would not go that far to label our activity as 'Stealing'. It is called containment of an asset with potential to promote the interest of civil society' John corrected.

'Okay. John, whatever you say. But, how do we move forward from here?'

'Hang on a sec. Let me figure it out' John said, dialing someone on the phone. He moved out of the room and returned a few minutes later.

'We are going to get a Portable Stone cutting laser device up here. But, it will take a day to get the equipment. We need to power it up with a make-shift battery. By the way, why the heck did they set such a stone inside the statue?' asked John.

'People who owned these pieces of Chintamani had developed superior nature apparently. The stone empowered them to think and act like Gods. Surya Varman apparently wanted everyone in his kingdom to pray to him and treat him like God. That is why he had set the stone at the base of the pedestal and made the statue the resembled him. It must be noted that both of them were extremely popular and they were never defeated in their lifetimes. They had become the centers of power as long as they ruled.' Vicky observed.

Lisa was skeptical. 'I can argue that Alexander, Adolf Hitler, Benito Mussolini, Josef Stalin and Fidel Castro also had or have similar mindset. They firmly believed that they had the divine right to rule and considered themselves to be above the Humanity'

'Yes. Lisa. You are right.' Vicky agreed 'But something else would have triggered their psychology. For instance, when Julius Caesar went to conquer Egypt, he had fallen head over heel when he saw Cleopatra. She made Caesar believe that he would be a fool to report to the Senate. She taught him the concept of the divine right of the ruler. Julius Caesar went back to Greece and showed his new megalomaniacal attitude. He was stabbed for that. Rest is History'

'You know what Vicky? You need a break. There is a good waterfall by name 'Ratannakiri' People go there to find Gemstones that wash out in the mud of the river. There is a dirt mud track for motor cycle riding. Lisa told me that you are an expert rider. You disappear for couple of days and we will have the stone ready here' John said.

'No John. I will just spend time in making the retrieval easy by energizing water. This will make the retrieval easy. By the way the waterfalls' actual name should have been 'Ratnagiri'. The name means 'Hill of Gemstones'. But, I think I will visit it when I am in a better frame of mind'

John lifted both his hands up making a gesture and walked out.

Couple of days later at night John sent couple of local men to drop a few innocuous pieces of small match box sized cartons near the sentry post. Ten minutes later he walked through the post. They guards were sound asleep. Using flash lights and battery lamps the team moved in.

Vicky sprinkled the sacred water all over the place and bathed the statue with it. Cool breeze began to blow soothingly. They retrieved the stone from the stone pedestal within an hour and drove away. Their next destination was Indonesia.

CHAPTER: FORTY EIGHT

If the Europeans and the regional despots tried hard to erase every aspect of Hindu roots in Asia, the Indonesians embraced it whole-heartedly. Indonesia, in spite of being the country with World's largest Muslim population, the people breathed and lived Hindu traditions.

'Garuda' is the National Airliner of Indonesia. The advertisement runs as 'Garuda—Vishnu Vahana'. India had been shamefully apologetic of its Hindu religion. The curse of India has been its leaders, who were at the helm of affairs when it won its Independence. As he repeatedly argued, Nehru was an agnostic and in fact he believed in Buddhism. Everything King Asoka did was glorified, such as the Buddha Stupa, the Asoka Chakra which became the National symbols.

The currency notes of Indonesia carried the image of 'Ganesha'. In India, the currency notes have the picture of Mohandas Gandhi, the one who preached against the principle of earning wealth. Gandhi wanted to subdue Hindu pride. Both Nehru and Gandhi understood the mentality of the British. They knew that they would be promoted and entertained by the British as long as they preached non-violence and guaranteed safety and security to the British living in India.

The hypocrisy of 'non-violence' was not lost on Vicky. As a school student he had once asked his History teacher, 'How can Gandhi support the British in the Second World War? If he was a true champion of non-violence, he must have supported anyone going to war.'

Vicky was completely fascinated by Indonesia.

The Capital City 'Jakarta' was actually 'Jayakartha' or 'The harbinger of victory'. Most of the words in Bahasa Indonesia originated from Sanskrit. In the island of Bali named after 'Vali' of Ramayana, where the majority of the population was Hindus, a few learned scholars spoke fluent Sanskrit. In Jogjakarta, there is a temple dedicated to the Hindu Trinity.—Brahma, the Creator, Shiva the destroyer and Vishnu, the protector, as is the order proclaimed only in the Vedas as 'Sa Brahma, Sa Siva Sa hari'. Otherwise, elsewhere the order of Brahma, Vishnu and Shiva was followed. In this temple, every full moon night, certain scenes of Ramayana are enacted in full glory which ends with the 'Lanka dahana' or the burning of Lanka. Like rest of South Asia, the Hindu epics of

Ramayana and Mahabharata are the two main epics around which Indonesian culture revolved.

Hinduism was brought to this country of over 13,000 islands by Maharishi Markandeya a Sage in Hindu epics. Although Hindu kingdoms existed since time immemorial, the recorded history significantly portrays kingdoms of Matram, Kadiri, Singhasari and Majapahit and Sri Vijaya of Sumatra. All these kingdoms were ruled by Hindu Kings and they had very powerful armies and prosperous kingdoms.

The third king of Kediri, Jayabhaya ruled in the 12th Century. He had the Royal Sign of 'Narasimha' or the 'Lion Incarnation of Lord Vishnu'. He leads a pious life and meditated in the forest and obtained supernatural powers. He considered himself to be one of the incarnations of Lord Vishnu. He had developed Super Natural powers and he had the capacity to look into the future. He wrote a book of prophesies called 'Pralembang Joyoboyo' in which he predicted the occupation of Indonesia by the Dutch and liberation of Indonesia by the Japanese during Second World war.

There is a temple dedicated to Raja Jayabaya in Bali and there is another temple dedicated to him at the remote mountain sanctuary Pura Pucak Penulisan. According to Kejawen Hindu belief, the Great Presidents of Indonesia, Sukarno and Suharto both meditated at this place to obtain Jayabaya's blessings and his supernatural powers and guidance. It is rumored that in the recent past,

President Abdurrahman Wahid also meditated at this place.

There is also a legend of Nyayi Roro Kidur. She was a Princess who was cursed and once she jumped into the South Ocean, she was cleared of the curse. She became a Mermaid Angel. President Suharto had instructed a Star Hotel, Hotel Samudera Indonesia to allot a separate luxury room to her. Every Thursday night, she would visit this room and eat the food served. An American wanted to take a photograph of her and he hid himself and waited. Next day morning, he was found dead and the photos when exposed turned out to be completely blank. The Hindu culture and traditions are deeply rooted in the psyche of Indonesians, so much so that in recent years, many people are getting 'converted' on their own accord to Hinduism and many Hindu temples are being revived for worship in Indonesia.

Secularism was supposed to keep the State away from the Religion. But, in India, the pseudo-secularists wanted to crush the Hindu thought and promote the other religions for two reasons—for their votes and to be seen as 'modern' and 'civil'. The disease spread to the so called 'Liberals' in India including a section of English media, who provoke level-headed Hindus by promoting writers who write vulgar things about Hindu Goddesses or promoting M.F.Husain, a sexual pervert who painted Hindu Goddesses nude. In spite of this, there are some insensitive actors in the film industry who felt proud to be the subject of his paintings.

India is a country of contradictions. Blasphemy is confused with freedom of expression. This is the country in which Dr.Yarlagadda gets Sahitya Akademi Award for writing a blasphemous book on the most respected and revered Goddess Draupadi. He had done it to become famous overnight. But, when Hindus protested, some sections of the media called them 'Right wing Hindu extremists' India is also a strangely highly tolerant country where the mentally sick pseudo secularists awarded Sunil Gangopadhaya—a writer who wrote many dirty things and openly admitted that he lusted after Goddess Saraswati, the Goddess of learning—an award of 'Saraswati Samman'. The Government had instituted a literary award in his name.

CHAPTER: FORTY NINE

After landing at Soekarno-Hatta International airport at Jakarta, Vicky and his team mates were greeted cordially by Damayanti from the US Embassy. She would be the liaison officer who would look after all their arrangements.

Indonesians had many names of Hindu origin, Such as Damayanti, Putri, Megawati, Dewi, Nila, Nirmala, Apsara and Rati. As they drove to Hotel Indonesia Kempinski, Damayanti explained various important buildings of Jakarta.

There was a statue of Lord Krishna and Arjuna from Mahabharata at the busiest intersections of Jakarta city.

'This is the largest statue of Krishna and Arjuna in the world. They are the characters from Mahabharata'

'Yes. I know' said Vicky.

But Vicky's 'Yes. I know' phrases stopped when she showed them the Defense Head Quarters of Indonesia. It was titled 'Yuddha Graha' an apt Sanskrit title. What was more revealing were the letters inscribed in Marble on the archway 'Chatur Dharma, Eka Karma'.

Down the road, she showed them the Ministry of Sports and the building had the name 'Krida Bhakti' or the 'Devotion to Sports'

There was a huge idol of Ganesa in front of the Presidential palace. Damayanti remarked 'Such statues are found in many Government offices and places in this country. Ganesha removes obstacles and brings good luck'

Soon, they arrived at the Hotel. It had two huge towers. Damayanti said 'This tower is called 'Ramayana tower' and the other one is called 'Ganesa tower. This Hotel is rebuilt over an older building Hotel Indonesia. It had the restaurant 'Ramayana' and a Permit room by name 'Ganesa' So, as we are proud of our culture and heritage, we named the towers after those names.

'If only our leaders in India had similar values' Vicky wondered.

Indonesian men wore Batik shirts as a tradition. Many of the dresses in Indonesia had traditional images of Garuda and Nagas. These two icons of Garuda, the Eagle vehicle of Lord Vishnu and Naga, the holy serpent had been the mainstay of everything Vicky had been observing in the past few days. They established a strong connection between the ancient Mayans and Hindu civilizations of South East Asia.

The following day, they were scheduled to take a short flight to the city of Solo or Sukarta. It was near Solo that the ancient temple of 'Candi Sukuh' was located on the western slopes of Mount Lawu near Solo. The approach road to the hill was very steep. After that, they walked to the temple.

Vicky was dumb struck when he saw the temple. It was the replica of 'Chichen Itza' of Mexico with a similar pyramid. There was a statue of 'Kurma' which was the incarnation of Lord Vishnu in form of a Turtle. He walked around and was aghast to witness the explicit symbolism of Vama Tantra. The place had many beheaded statues of naked men. The temple was once dedicated to Bhima, one of the Pandavas. He found the images of Ganesa and Lord Shiva on the walls.

The image of Ganesa had close resemblance with the description in Tibetan Buddhist Tantra. A spike of chill ran up Vicky's spine. He experienced shortness of breath and his head ached badly. His feeling of demonic possession was coming back to him.

The Burmese brothers had already started the work with the infra red cameras. He walked towards Lisa and said 'I am not feeling too well. I need to rest. I cannot stay here for long'

'What's wrong Vicky?'

'I don't know. But, please excuse me. I am going to sit outside this place'. Vicky walked out of the complex. He could hear whispers and slight laughter. He turned back to see if it was Lisa or John. They were all standing away from each other. He immediately understood that it was his brain that was playing tricks. He closed his eyes and went into meditation.

He felt something touching his head. He opened his eyes and was shocked to see a person with red blood colored eyes and a long beard wearing a garland of skulls. He had placed a human thigh bone on Vicky's head.

He spoke 'So, Vikram, you are here for Chintamani stone' in chaste Telugu.

'Who are you? How do you know my mother tongue Telugu'. Vicky found difficult to speak.

'I know everything. Listen carefully. Do not disturb this site. You will be in danger. Do not take any stone from this place. This place is cursed. It belongs to a famous Vama Tantrik by name 'Kukaraja' or 'King of Dogs' who performed Ganacakra in a burial ground in the nights. Many evil spirits haunt this place."

'What should we now?'

'What you are looking for is not here. It has been removed long back from this place. The Chintamani stone was brought here from the temple of Jayabhaya. Many years ago, it has been stolen by the powerful Tantrik Raktakapala to a village near a city called Balik papan in Kalimantan'

'Who are you?' asked Vicky.

'I was once his Master. I had taught him the Tantra that is used for the good of the mankind. He started praying to strong tantric forces and has obtained Chintamani stone. He is very powerful now and has occult powers'

'How do we subdue him and take the stone?'

'You need to perform Katuka fire ritual to gain overpower his occult. I cannot do it as it requires undisturbed recital of the chants for 4 hours with utmost concentration. You have the power to perform this. We have no time to lose Vikram. We will go to my house now and you must start this immediately. It is New moon night in two days and Raktakapala would go into meditation and know about this. He will then perform worship to Nikhumbhila and wear Chintamani stone to become invincible. We need to vanquish him before tomorrow nightfall"

After an hour, Vicky was given the initiation into the chant. John and Lisa made arrangements for their trip to Balik Papan.

CHAPTER: FIFTY

The same day they flew back to Jakarta. Vicky was running high temperature. Throughout the journey, he went into deep sleep.

To reach Balik Papan on a Thursday was not just a mistake. It was a disaster in waiting. Damayanti for all her knowledge about Indonesia did not know about the danger she was putting her guests into.

The 30 seater Garuda landed in the morning in Balikpapan and they found just 5 taxis waiting. Except for Vicky and the team, the plane was empty except for a Church father. They hopped into two taxis. The taxi drivers objected taking Vicky.

'He is wearing Black shirt and we cannot risk it' said one taxi driver.

'Why? What is the problem?' protested Damayanti.

'The curse will fall upon us if we discuss. Please understand. This Gentleman must change his cloths'

Vicky pulled out a white tee shirt from his bag and put it on. He did not want to tax his brain arguing with them.

'Another request, Please maintain absolute silence until we reach the city as it is Thursday today' said the driver.

After a few minutes the road passed through a village. Vicky was aghast when he saw hut after hut circled by live raging fires. But the fire did not touch the hut made with dry thatched leaves. In front of each hut were a person and his family. A large skull and bones were placed in front of the person and another person was jumping up in the air and dancing and falling down. This was the ubiquitous scene throughout the village. No one spoke a word.

When the cars reached the Balik papan Novotel, Vicky felt he had entered another world—the world of reality. He felt home in the luxurious lobby of the Hotel. He sulked down on a leather sofa and closed his eyes. Minutes later, he checked in and received his room key card.

'I need a Tourist Guide' he asked the Front Desk.

'We can help you with one. He is a freelancer and he charges US $ 50 per day'

288

'It is okay. How soon can I have him here?'

'In an hour'

'Thanks. Please send him to my room'

Vicky felt ravenous hungry. He ordered 'Nasih Goreng' and 'Ayam Goreng' which literally meant 'Fried Rice' and 'Friend Chicken'.

He called Damayanti, John and Lisa to his room. He wanted them to meet the tourist guide. He wanted to know lot of answers.

A few minutes later, a tall and stout person knocked the door.

'I am Sudirman, the Tourist Guide' he introduced.

'Please do come in' Vicky offered a chair.

Vicky inquired about the villages that he had seen on the way to the City. He wanted to know where he could find Raktakapala.

The moment he heard the name, Sudirman searched for an Ashtray. 'I hope this is a smoking room'

'Yes. Here is your ashtray' Vicky offered.

'What I am going to tell you can get me killed. Raktakapala is the most dreaded Black Magician of Indonesia. He does not live in a particular village. He wanders around and he does most of his Black Magic during nights in burial grounds. He carries a big skull supposedly that of his Master from which he drinks blood'

John interrupted 'I thought Cannibals were either in Sumatra or Irian Jaya. So, is this guy a Cannibal?'

'No sir. I am not aware of that. But, the locals fear him a lot. He sometimes goes to a village and demands a young virgin girl. He demands that all the virgin girls be brought forward. He would select one girl and take her away. A few days later, someone would find pieces of her dress drenched in blood.'

'Then what the heck is your Government doing about this guy?' John asked.

'No one had the courage to register a complaint. Those who tried to do so, died under mysterious circumstances. This terrorized the people here. He has Supernatural powers.' Sudirman took a deep pull on his clove cigarette.

John said 'Vicky. I am surprised that your old guy at the hill temple got this guy's name right. So, if he was right about his name, he should be right that he has the stone with him'

'What stone sir?' Sudirman asked.

'Nothing, Now tell me about the village. What are those fires and why the fire did not burn down the huts and who were those people dancing?'

'Sir, you have been through one of the villages that are deeply indulged in black magic. They invoke spirits into one of their family members and appease them with food. Mostly their ancestral spirits are invoked. It happens only on Thursdays. It is a dangerous to travel on Thursdays in those places'

Damayanti asked 'So, how can we search for Raktakapala?'

Sudirman got up and said 'You have to go to every burial ground around Balikpapan tonight. Today, being Thursday, he will do his Tantra until the early hours of Friday.' Suddenly, Sudirman's hand started shaking. 'Are you not interested in tourist attractions in the area?' he asked.

'No. We are here only for Raktakapala'

'Okay. But I think no taxi will take you to these places. I have to bring my car. But, I will charge you extra'

John said 'We will pay you whatever you want man.'

'Ok. I will wait for you at the lobby. It is already six now. We can start in half an hour'. Sudirman left.

CHAPTER: FIFTY ONE

They reached the lobby and found Sudirman stretching his head back on the sofa and closing his eyes. Damayanti asked one of the bell boys to wake him up. The Bell boy tried his best. Sudirman would not wake up. He was dead.

The Hotel Manager rushed to the spot and he immediately moved his body to his office which was by the side. He did not want the news of a dead man in the lobby. Bad publicity was not welcome. So, he called the Police.

This is the second death he has seen in pursuit to unravel the mystery of Chintamani. Vicky said 'I am not feeling good about this John. You need to get your Agency's contacts here. I don't think we have much time. The cab driver has given the name of the village'

'Yes Vicky. I think this guy has a deep cult following. If you want to meet him and talk to him then it's a different story. But if you want him dead, it's a cake walk for us. Just give me four hours and that bastard is dead meat. I can get our Boys from Makatur base in action within couple of hours. But we got to figure out this weasel lives in.'

'It is very reassuring to know that. I hope the Indonesian Government would mind if your troops are involved. We hope we can retrieve the stone from him'

'Relax Vicky. Before you sleep tonight, you will have the stone' John walked away to his room.

Vicky and others were asked a few questions by the Police. They attributed Sudhirman's death due to natural causes.

Vicky, Lisa, John and a group of 4 commandoes got into 2 SUV trucks and headed towards the village of Kampong Sayur. The village is in a deep jungle area. From a distance a huge dome like structure was visible. As they approached nearer, the image of a huge monster was visible on the dome.

Suddenly there was a sound of a big boom and a huge pulse wave struck both the vehicles lifting them in the air and hurling the giant SUVs several feet away. Vicky and John got badly bruised. The commandos in the other SUV got out and started firing and charged towards the dome building. Vicky pocketed the holy water and ran along with the commandos. Just as they entered the front yard an 8 feet giant appeared and roared with laughter. He was

Raktakapala. Before anyone could assess the situation, he held his hand to the front and everyone fell down unconscious including Vicky.

When he regained consciousness, he realized that he and the others were chained to a grill railing. Raktakapala was seated facing the sacrificial fire and directly in front of him was Lisa naked and in a state of trance. Raktakapala's disciples brought a huge sword and placed it beside him. He continued chanting verses and throwing offerings into the fire.

Vicky realized that he has very little time on his hands. If he poured the holy water into the fire, it will certainly stop the ritual. The American commandos are trained to break the hand cuffs and chains. One commando freed himself and rushed and attacked Raktakapala.

Vicky plunged ahead and poured the water in the fire. Raktakapala gave out a chilling shriek. He fell on the ground and beat his limbs on the ground. His entire face turned black and black blood oozed out of his mouth. His power was neutralized. He could not sustain the attack of the commandos. He breathed his last. Lisa was shaken back into consciousness. She ran into a corner and put on her cloths.

It took a few seconds for the reality to sink in. The commandos retook the possession of weapons. The disciples of Raktakapala took to their heels. Vicky found the Chintamani piece of stone in Raktakapala's chambers. It had developed a dark tint.

Vicky was excited that the mission had finally come to an end. He will go back to the United States and continue his research and co-relate all the stones and find the secret behind the Chintamani. An hour later, the entire team was in a jeep en route to the city. The last sight of Raktakapala's was a gruesome—that of a horrific giant with big eyes and beard and garland of skulls. He had tattoos all over his body and wore dark red clothes. His body was on the floor and was drilled with perhaps dozens of bullets that the commandoes pumped in to make no room for surprises.

He checked the stone again. It was Dark Green Black combination in color. He handed over the stone to Lisa.

That night he slept without any nightmares. It was 3:00 am when the phone rang again. It was Lisa on the phone

'Vicky. Hurry up. We have to go right now. We haven't got much time.'

'What is the problem now?'

'John had a call from Langley, way from the top. They want you and me in Washington in the next 24 hours. There is a crisis that is emerging. I will meet you in the lobby in five minutes' Lisa sounded a bit panicky.

Vicky stashed his clothes in his bag and quickly washed his face and ran to the elevator. Lisa was waiting for him. A person in military uniform snatched his bag

'Let's go. Let's go' he said

Vicky and Lisa rushed out and jumped into the jeep. In a few minutes, they found themselves in front of a helicopter. The chopper belonged to the Indonesian Military. They flew to the airport where a private jet was waiting for them.

All this seemed to be dream world to Vicky 'I did not get to even say Thanks to John' he said.

'It's okay Vicky. He understands. You can call him from Washington'

They landed in Jakarta airport and were rushed immediately to a Washington bound Commercial aircraft that had been kept on the taxiway just for them.

'Here are your boarding cards for First Class' a young lady handed over the cards to Vicky and Lisa

They mumbled thanks and climbed up the plane. Ultimate luxury and serenity marked the First Class cabin of Garuda. An old professor like person in the next seat looked daggers at Vicky.

'So you are the Heroes we are all waiting for' he remarked.

Vicky sat silently and fastened his seat belt. He had a long and tiring day.

CHAPTER: FIFTY TWO

The first class has a fully stretched out bed in a small cubicle. If one had to talk to another passenger, it needed one to stretch forward. Unlike the fully closed cabins that are in vogue, Garuda had a partition half way up. It offered privacy as well a feeling of open space.

The guy who was sitting beside him was talking to Lisa. Vicky freshened up in the Water Closet and the stewardess asked him if he liked Coffee.

'American Espresso' Vicky said. He also chose his meal from the Menu.

Lisa introduced Vicky.

'This is Vicky my colleague. This is Jack Angels. He is an Art dealer and has a chain of Premium stores in the United States'.

299

'How do you do Jack and sorry about yesterday's hold up'

'No problem at all'

Vicky went back to his seat and his meal was brought. He ate up to his heart's content.

Jack looked at him and said 'We have 12 more hours to kill'

'Yes. But I am refreshed now. I am a Professor from India. I am curious to know more about your nature of Business. Do you find many people who are interested in Asian art?'

'Of course. People are interested in exotic stuff all the time you know. But, the key to the success of my business is that in-depth knowledge on history and culture of Asia'

'That puts us pretty close in our profession, although slightly different. I am working on Noetic science and it also involves religion amongst other disciplines.'

'Which countries have you been touring?' asked Jack

'Since a few days, I have been touring Thailand, Cambodia and Indonesia and I am surprisingly shocked to see the connection between Hindu India and these countries. I also explored the deep connection with Mexican Maya civilization with ancient India'

'Good. You should also explore the connection in Malaysia, Philippines and Japan. Malaysia has many people of Indian origin'

'I am aware of the connection between India and Malaysia. The name 'Malaya' originated from Tamil language 'Malai' or 'Hill'. The Chief of Military is called as Lakshmana, with respect to Rama's brother Lakshmana in Ramayana. There are many temples in Malaysia and the Indian influence is obvious. Singapore is derived from 'Singa Pura' or 'the City of Lions.

Vicky continued, 'But Japan? I am not aware of any ancient Indian cultural or religious connected between India and Japan.'

'Take a look at this catalog. These paintings depict Gods who look similar to Hindu Gods. But they have Japanese names'

The goddess of learning Saraswati was depicted as 'Benzaiten' or 'Benten'. The god of war 'Kartikeya' was depicted as 'Bishamonten'. Ganesha was depicted as 'Shoten Kangiten'. 'Daikoku' is the name the Japanese gave to Shiva, whereas Vishnu was depicted as the harbinger of protection and welfare and protector of their fishermen in form of 'Ebisu'. 'Jurogin' is the Japanese version of 'Brahma' the creator. Goddess 'Lakshmi' who the ancient Europeans prayed to as 'Lakme' was 'Kichijoten' for the Japanese. Kubera is prayed to as 'Hotei' by the Japanese. Most of these deities adorned the Shinto temples across Japan. Literally, the Japanese religion harnessed the positive power of the Hindu deities.

'This is quite interesting. I see a remarkable similarity between the Hindu deities and the Shinto Gods of Japan. I must visit Japan someday to further explore the connection between these two great civilizations. I had been to The Philippines last year. Archeologists and Historians strongly believe that there is a deep connection between India and that country. It was called Panyupayana. There are similarities between Telugu script and that of Filipino. The capital city 'Manila' is derived from Manu, who had written the Law books in Hindu literature. The Philippines Parliament building has the statue of Manu with the inscription below 'The first, the Greatest and the wisest lawgiver of Mankind'. The national flower of Philippines is the Indian Champaka flower.'

'I think the ancient Indian culture covers almost entire globe'

Vicky continued 'Yes Jack. Going further south, Australia also has deep connection with ancient India. Scientists have discovered recently that a particular gene, Holocene of the aborigines and that of Indians is common and the migration started occurring more than 20,000 years ago. The aborigine leaders are called 'Gurus' which is a Sanskrit word. The area of Gympie near Brisbane is named as 'Merundai', which takes its name from Mount Meru. The South Pole was called 'Dakshina Meru' by the ancient

Hindus. The aborigines of Australia and the civilization of Southern India followed the similar practices of praying to village goddesses. They follow similar rituals. Many names of the places in Australia are based on Sanskrit language.'

'I read that the ancient Indian culture had spread more predominantly about 5,000 years ago' mentioned Jack.

'Yes Jack. The past 5,000 years has witnessed a fresh wave of new settlements. Arjuna, the Hero of Hindu epic Mahabharath conquered lands what we know today as Argentina. As Silver was a predominant metal in the area, the word silver itself took the name 'Argentum' in Latin, named after 'Arjuna'.

'Why did the Hindu civilization decline worldwide? It's a mystery that a faith with long history finally was restricted to only India'

'The ancient Hindus from India were great seafarers. There came about a period when the most talented migrated to overseas Hindu colonies. To arrest this alarming rate of exodus, some narrow minded priests have misinterpreted ancient texts and proclaimed that those in the learned class, who cross the ocean will face immediate expulsion from the society. This dealt a death blow to the Hindu settlements all around the world. Over a period of time, all these countries were subject to hordes of preachers of other religions and the grand Hindu temples were either destroyed or converted mostly into Buddhist monasteries. Jack, the greatness of Hindu way

303

of life is that it is essentially is a non-violent and peace loving in nature. It permits the followers to pray to any deity or respect and follow any faith. But the bane of the Sanatana Religion is that it does not have a specific unitary controlling authority like the Pope for Catholics. This let some vested interests to distort the truth and lead to many dogmas and meaningless practices and traditions.'

CHAPTER: FIFTY THREE

Lisa was nervous. Vicky sat beside her and in a very low voice asked her 'Any news Lisa? Can you give me more information on as to why we being called on Emergency basis to Washington?'

'I don't have any idea Vicky. But, trust me. By the way the arrangements have been made to get us back, there must have been a huge development.'

'Let us watch some news'. Vicky took the earphones and toggled the Personal Entertainment System to get the news capsule.

On CNN, he watched a report. 'North Korean Leader Kim Jong-Un today issued an unequivocal and direct threat to the United States that DPRK shall conduct a pre-emptive strike against it. He spoke of realizing the dream of a unified Korea. Meanwhile, the nuclear warhead missile was moved into the missile launch site. It is known that North Korea had nuclear devices but the expelled IAEA officials say that it did not have the sufficient plutonium enrichment materials. In the other news . . .'

Vicky spent a few minutes toggling the channels. Then, he went back to his seat and recapitulated what had happened and what could the connection be. He went into a wakeful sleep. Again he dreamt about struggling alone on the snowy plain and meeting the holy person. He now started worrying about his irregular sleeping pattern. When he went to the washroom to freshen up, he saw a dry clot of blood in his nostril. For the first time in his life, he was concerned about his health.

A few hours later, the plane landed in Dulles International Airport in Washington D.C. The moment the plane landed, two black suited men entered the plane and escorted Lisa and Vicky out. Their baggage was kept by the stewardess and the airlines staff helped with the bags. They were immediately put on a chopper.

Lisa asked 'Where are we going'

'The White House'

They were escorted to the West Wing directly to a room. The bags were given to them.

One of the officers came in and said, 'Vicky and Lisa. You have 5 minutes to get into the meeting. You can change your dress. If you have suit you better wear them as you will be meeting the President.'

If this was a dream for Lisa, it was a dream that came at the wrong time for Vicky. He will not have answer to a single question that might be put to him. What kind of expertise can he give? If he is meeting the President of the United States, the most powerful Man in the World, he better answer with some smartness.

He changed into his favorite dark green suit. He had not shaved he realized. But there was no time for shaving. He sprayed his favorite Pour Homme 'Drakker Noir'

Lisa entered the room in a suit. The door opened. Lisa's face brightened up as he saw Agent Stephen.

'Hi Lisa, Come with me'

They walked into the conference room. The entire scene was intimidating. The Defense Secretary and the Secretary of State entered.

The General stood up. 'Okay Ladies and Gentleman. We have a situation here that has a proclivity of becoming a full blown International crisis. American interests are at stake here. The President has called this emergency meeting. The President is expected here anytime now'

President Peterson entered the room with his assistant and the Chief of Staff. Everyone rose. 'Please sit Gentlemen . . . and Ladies'.

'So, tell me what I need to know' he looked straight at the General. The military officer began 'We have been observing unusual activity in the North Korean nuclear Yongbyan nuclear facility for the past 72 hours. This is after the missile has been moved to the launch site. These are the images taken by our Geo Stationary Satellite. They clearly indicate DPRK restarting its Plutonium enrichment activity.'

'As I remember, we and South Korea have sabotaged this capability. How did they manage to get on feet so quickly?' asked the President.

'Mr. President. Our Comint and Sigint suggests that the North Koreans are in possession of a hyper-catalyst material that can reprocess the spent Plutonium in matter of hours. Our South Korean counterparts have mentioned this as a very unique substance going by the name of Chintamani stone. This is the same stone that stolen from us a few weeks ago from Rixton University. This was discovered in some ancient temple ruins in Mexico a few weeks back. Assistant Professor Jennifer Corning was beheaded and the stone was moved to the North Koreans by a guy whose name according to our records is Lee Dixon and his real name is Lee Ho Hung.'

'Do you have any scientific corroboration that this stone has the capabilities to accelerate processing of a nuclear material?' the President asked.

'Sir, we are trying to figure that out. We have just obtained the possession of three similar stones thanks to the co-ordinated efforts of the Bureau and the Agency and the Professor from India, Mr. Vikram. They collected them from various temples in South East Asia'

FBI agent Stephen was holding the boxes. He opened them and placed the three stones on the table. Two of them shone bright and the third shone with dark tint.

The stones were extremely bright. The sight was awe-inspiring. The stones seemed to have a mesmerizing affect.

The President looked at the stones for a few moments and turned to Vicky.

'So, tell me Professor. What do you think? What is the specialty of these stones?'

'Mr. President. It will be difficult for the Science community and any rational person to believe what I am going to say. I believe these stones are the material that can accentuate the power of human beings or energize inorganic matter. If you have a few minutes, I want to explain a theory which will put the things in the right perspective'

'Go ahead' said the President.

CHAPTER: FIFTY FOUR

'I have developed this theory. I named it as 'The Theory of Super Human Evolution'. The premise of this theory is that as Homo Sapiens have evolved from apes, it is a natural eventuality that this process of evolution continues and Humans will end up as Super Humans in future. However, some of us have the capability of evolving much faster than others. To understand this, we use a yard stick which I call HCI or Human Capability Index. I use a mathematical function with variables of Mental, Physical and Spiritual strengths, equivalent to that of an average human being and fix this value as digit 1. People sitting in this room are far more capable and talented compared to a normal human being. So, their HCI index would be somewhere above 1 and less than 10.'

Vicky drank some water and continued.

'Hindu mythology suggests that an ancient entity by name Ravan was in possession of the original unbroken Chintamani stone. What you see are just the outer shell fragments of that original stone. Ravan in my theory had HCI index of 10. He was also called the 10 headed Demon. Now, if we apply this to inorganic or electromagnetic material or thermo nuclear material or nuclear fuels, this stone has the extra-ordinary ability to accelerate that process. It has extreme positive energy and the material transcends this acceleration characteristic across 10 dimensions of the Universe, as is postulated in the String theory'

'Impressive. Now tell me. How could the North Koreans be aware of this stone?'

'Mr. President. The Koreans also have a lot of commonality with Indians. There was a Princess by name Heo from Ayodhya who migrated to Korea in the 1st Century and married the king there. Around 6 million Koreans share the same gene pool with Indians and it's been proven through DNA tests. There are some ancient tribes in Korea who pray to Hindu Gods and ancient temples were unearthed recently. Evidently, some of these Hindu cults might have the followers in the DPRK probably in the higher ranks. Once they knew about the discovery of Chintamani stone, they stole it and probably would have tested it and now they are successfully using it to enrich their Plutonium'

'So, now tell me how can you destroy this material?'

'This material is supposed to demonstrate the strongest trait of Quantum entanglement theory. Essentially, this means that one part of the stone can influence the other part. Although these small stones are placed tens of thousands of miles away, they are all connected. I understand the piece that the North Koreans have stolen, is the outer shell of the original Chintamani stone. As this material transcends the 10 dimensions, all the pieces are in fact connected and act as a singular unit. I can say that these stones are relatively duller now compared to what I had observed them to be when they were in Asia. Their energy strength has slightly diminished. This makes me believe that we are father away from its source of power, the nucleus of the stone. Like the Magnet pieces head towards North, these pieces point towards the Himalayas. People like Roerich believed that the actual stone is a place called Shambhala in the Himalayas. So, if we can destroy the source, we destroy the power of these fragments and they will be nothing but mere paper weights'

The President turned towards his Secretary of Defense.

'Tell me. What are our military options and risks?'

'Mr. President. If we do not stop the North Koreans now, it will be too late. DPRK has the missile on launch site and it can attack the United States in matter of hours. I suggest a pre-emptive air strike on Pyongyang and also at Yongbyan that can neutralize their capabilities.'

He turned to the Secretary of state. 'The South Koreans say that that is exactly the kind of excuse DPRK would want to launch a full scale war. The South sees that Kim Jong-Un will see an air strike by the Americans as an act of war and will attack Seoul first. South Korea will win the war. But, millions of lives are at stake here. Eventually, the North Korean people will cross the 38th Parallel and flood South Korea and cripple their economy. They do not want such an outcome.'

'What are our diplomatic options?'

'Mr. President, Ever since the United States has gone back on the 'Agreed Framework' there is huge amount of Trust deficit between the countries. I am sure that the North Koreans will love to talk to us. But, they will give us nothing and in turn will black mail us and the South Koreans to giving into their demands. I suggest that we take some kind of a neutralizing action—military or otherwise. Diplomacy wins when we the opponent has something to lose if talks fail. Right now, the North Koreans have nothing to lose'

'All right, I give Prof. Vikram and his team 100 hours to neutralize this thing. If you fail, I am going to order a full scale annihilation of the site' The President stood up.

Then he walked towards Vicky and shook his hand. 'Good Luck Professor'

'Sir, I will do my best'. Then the President left along with his men.

Prof. Conrad spoke 'Vicky. I am impressed. Now, you have the job cut out. You have to find the answers. What else did you decipher from the plank?'

'Professor, I have a reason to believe that the actual stone is in India in the Himalayas. I think I have to go there immediately. Do we have the budget for this mission?'

'Don't worry about Budget Vicky. I am going to give you a Charge card of our Agency. You can buy a Chopper and blow it up with the kind of money you can draw with that card and no questions asked' Agent Stephen said with a smile.

'Thank you Stephen. I appreciate it'

Stephen opened his bag and gave Vicky an envelope containing the charge card. 'The PIN number is in it as well'

'Hang on a sec' Stephen gestured and he took out a pouch containing a satellite phone. 'This is for you Vicky. Now you stay connected wherever you are. Good luck' He handed it to Vicky and left the room.

CHAPTER: FIFTY FIVE

He thought about the daunting task ahead of him He started to change his perspective. If he succeeds in his mission, he would save millions of lives. He needed strength. He needed support. No Human can give it to him. He needed God's love. He needed God's guidance. Today, he needed God to be with him as a friend. For all the religious fervor since his childhood, Vicky struck a chord with the fact that he badly was in need of with the Almighty. He felt being part of God and God loved him more because he has now grown out of petty give and take relationship with him.

'You will catch the night's flight to New Delhi. You will be accompanied by Lisa.' Stephen said.

'I have a request. I want to go to Pittsburg before that'

'Why? Any special reason' Agent Stephen asked.

317

'Yes. Its personal. I have to visit a Temple.'

'You don't have time to drive. You can use one of our choppers. Lisa, you go ahead and make the arrangements.' He got up from the chair and said

'Okay Professor. Give us some Good news. Take care Lisa' Stephen left the room.

The Venkateswara temple at Pittsburg is the replica of the Tirumala Temple, the richest and busiest temple in the world and one of Vicky's favorite. Vicky was emotionally overpowered looking at his Lord's idol. He asked God for strength, for his love and for his guidance. He sat in a corner of the front yard and meditated for 20 minutes. He gained calmness and the presence of God in his heart. 'With you in my heart my Lord, I can conquer anything' he said to himself and left the temple.

The Air India flight to New Delhi was over crowded. Vicky and Lisa did not speak much on the plane. He was oblivious of his surroundings. When he looked at the Menu, he felt a sudden revulsion to Chicken and meat. As Buddha said, it takes a moment for a person to change. That very moment Vicky renounced Non vegetarian food forever. He ordered Vegetarian food. Thankfully, the standards of Air India had improved tremendously. The food was superb.

Stretching his seat back, he ruminated on the course of action. In the plank, Vicky had observed the engraving of couple of temples in India. One was in Southern India and one was in Northern India. Prof. Sastry wrote to him identifying the temples as that of Tanjore in Tamilnadu, one of the largest temples in the world, bearing a five ton stone on top of its huge Tower. Tanjore temple was built by Raja Raja Chola to atone his sins for attacking Sri Lanka in pitch dark of midnight with arrows headed with burning cloths gaining a victory against every tenet of lawful warfare.

The temple in North India was that of Goddess Hidimbi in Himachal Pradesh. Hidimbi was a character in the Hindu epic, Mahabharata. She was the wife of Bheema the strongest of the Pandavas. According to the legend, Hidimbi wanted to offer Human sacrifice to appease Goddess. She sent her son Gatotkacha to bring a human being. His father Bheema chided him and Hidimbi for pursuing such degraded methods to appease Goddess. Then his son went to Indonesia and meditated there. There is a temple there dedicated to him. He obtained a secret stone which he presented it to his mother. She then obtained divinity and a temple was constructed in her name. People in Himachal Pradesh pray to her as an aspect of Divine Mother Goddess.

Vicky did not have much time to visit both these temples. There was nothing to gain by visiting these temples. He was sure that the original Chintamani stone was elsewhere.

He prayed silently seeking guidance and went into deep sleep.

'You are the chosen one. Come to me and I will guide you'

'But sir, who are you? Where do you live?' asked Vicky.

'I am Vishwa Dharma and I live in Motichur near Rishikesh'

The person in bright Saffron robe disappeared. Vicky suddenly sprang up in shock. He was dreaming. He perceived the message as a God given guidance.

He was eager for his plane to land in New Delhi. Delhi has been the capital of India for centuries. This area was the capital of the Pandavas during Mahabharata times. It was called as 'Indraprastha' Vishwa Dharma's ashram at Motichur was in vicinity to the holy town of Rishikesh which is one of the hubs of Hindu spirituality. But, Vicky did not have much knowledge of this place. So, he opened the debit card given to him and swiped it on the phone by his seat and called Prof. Sastry in Hyderabad, who after an hour provided the information.

The dream brought in a sense of clarity but also a sense of urgency in Vicky. He did not want to waste much time as Motichur was close to Delhi. Winters in Delhi is usually cruelly cold and the smog always gave the pilots lot of problems in landing and take-offs. It is only the pilots from Norway who are the best pilots of Commercial Aviation, as they were habituated to handle the planes in Norway which most of the times suffer from sub-zero temperatures and near-zero visibility.

The plane made a smooth landing at the Indira Gandhi International Airport. Air India has a strict rule that the pilots should not exceed 1.65 G while landing the aircraft. This is also the norm set by the Indian Government. But, the international norm permitted above 2.3o G which was the reason why most of the other airlines land with a thud. They complain of short runways and the practical factors for not adhering to the 1.65 G threshold.

Vicky and Lisa checked into Inter-continental Hotel as it was in proximity to the Airport and after a quick shower and breakfast engaged a cab to take them to Motichur.

In about 5 hours of drive, they arrived at Motichur. Vicky inquired for Vishwa Dharma. It was very easy to locate his ashram. Lisa was amazed at the fact that what Vicky had dreamt about was in fact a reality manifested as a dream.

When they reached the ashram, there were two monks waiting for them. They said 'Our Guruji is waiting for you'

As they entered the ashram, Vicky and Lisa were asked to remove their shoes and they walked bare foot to the front court yard where a Vishwa Dharma was standing.

'Come Vikram. You have no time to lose' he entered inside a room.

'Less than 200 kilometers from here, you will find a village by name Nagashanka. Once you enter the village, ask for

Chandra Sekhar Swami. He is my disciple. He is aware of your arrival here, as has the power to know everything. He is the only person who is capable of solving the problem'

'You will find help coming your way in a few moments. But, what you are going to attempt now has never been done before. Some powerful force will pose peril. I am trying this talisman around your wrist. This will protect you'

Vicky folded his hands as a mark of respect.

They left the ashram and walked toward the cab. Lisa then showed a small pod to Vicky. 'Vicky, let me explain this. This is a GPS device. If our satellite phone does not work, this will help our Head Quarters in the United States to keep us tracked. Look at this button here in red color and also this button in black color. If you press both these buttons for five seconds simultaneously that will trigger a distress call.'

Vicky counted the hours from the time President Peterson had given him the deadline of hundred hours. It was only forty hours ago.

CHAPTER: FIFTY SIX

Lisa's phone rang. It was from Washington. She was instructed to stand down as the Indian Government took the charge of this mission. Even before she disconnected the call, she could hear the sound of an approaching chopper.

The chopper approached them and a Marcos commando quickly jumped off the rope ladder and identified himself to Vicky and Lisa.

Marcos in India were equal to Navy Seals of the United States. They were trained to handle any combat situation. These rapid deployment crack team were deployed instantly during Mumbai attacks on 26/11.

The Americans, Europeans and the Israelis come to India to get trained in Jungle warfare and High Altitude warfare. India also maintains 3,000 combat troops on the world's highest combat zone, the Siachin Glacier where temperatures fall below 50 degrees centigrade. Indian soldiers are the best in High altitude and mountain warfare. The High Altitude Warfare School of Indian Army is considered to be one of the most elite military training centers on the planet.

"I am Captain Lakshman of Special Ops unit of Marcos, Indian Navy. I am leading this mission."

"How do you know about the mission sir" Vicky wondered.

'We have our ways and means Vicky. We don't have much time to lose. Get on to the chopper. We will go to Nagashankha village'

As they headed towards the village, a snow blizzard ensued. Visibility turned almost zero. The air turned thin and all that was visible on the ground was snow.

'Garuds, we should have brought Garuds on this mission' Lakshman rued. The Garuds are India's elite Air Commandos. They are some of the best chopper and aircraft pilots in the world'

Time lost its meaning and in a few seconds the chopper lost control and started losing the altitude. Parachutes were of no use at such a low level and there was no time. Vicky instinctively jumped out of the chopper and rolled over. The chopper eventually crashed with a loud thud just a few feet away from Vicky.

Captain Lakshman was badly bruised and his hand flesh had torn off. But he ordered 'First take Lisa out to safety' Two commandos scrambled out and pulled Lisa out and carried her away to safe zone. Lakshman let other two commandoes clear out. But he was stranded with the seat belt wrangling around his body. Vicky ran towards the chopper and with the help of the commandoes cut the belt and they dragged him out just in time before the chopper exploded and went up in flames.

It took Lisa ten minutes to realize what had transpired. She reached out to the GPS device and pressed the distress protocol. She looked out for Vicky. He was gone. She learnt from the commandos that he had walked towards the main road as he did not want to lose time.

'How are you feeling now sir?' Lisa asked Lakshman who was getting first aid.

'I will be fine Lisa. How are you?'

'I am fine sir. I have sent a distress call. We will get help soon'

In spite of the pain Lakshman gave out a big laughter. 'Much before your signal reached Washington, our C5—Clandestine Critical Communications & Command

Centre—in Delhi would have got the message through our flight instrumentation and help must be on the way.

'Did you ask your guys to pull me out of the chopper first. It was so courageous and generous of you. Thank you sir'

'There is nothing great about it Lisa. It is a part of Indian culture. We treat our guests with divine respect. We keep their honor and lives above ours, and talking of courage, what I did today is insignificant when you consider how our soldiers fought in Kargil war. Just as the Americans say 'Remember Alamo', we say 'Remember Saragarhi'. In 1898, twenty one Silk Soldiers faced 14,000 Afghan soldiers and killed many thousands of them. When they ran out of infantry, these brave soldiers fought with their hands and killed 800 Afghan soldiers before getting killed. There is no match in the history of mankind for such valor Lisa' Lisa was bewildered completely.

In a few seconds an Air Force Jet flew past them and on the return sortie it dropped a big bag. It contained a mini surgery kit, a tent, hot water, refreshments, warm clothing and many essentials. In less than hour two choppers arrived on search & rescue mission.

In the meantime, Vicky managed to spot a small freight truck and got into it. As religion flowed through his veins, he prayed to Muneeswara, the God who prevented road accidents. Almost everyone, who bought a new vehicle in his hometown Chennai, visited his shrine near the Central Railway station seeking protection against accidents.

His thoughts were suddenly interrupted by the driver. 'You have to take that direction. You must walk. There is no road.'

He zipped up his jacket and put on his cap. Ahead of him was a narrow path. As he walked, he tried to evade his thoughts. He spotted some houses at a distance and walked faster. He reached Nagashanka village.

Vicky spoke Hindi well. This is in spite of the fact that Chennai was famous for its anti-Hindi agitations in the past when the Government tried to make this language spoken by majority of Indians as a National language. But, those with cosmopolitan outlook learnt Hindi and it is also taught at the Central Board schools.

Although the villagers showed Vicky the direction to visit the cave of Chandra Swami, they were unwilling to let him go. The real spirit and culture of India lies in its villages. It takes only a few minutes for the villagers to take anyone as their honored guest and they feed and help the strangers.

'It's dangerous to visit the cave tonight. Why don't you sleep and go tomorrow morning?' cautioned an elderly villager.

'No sir. I am going now. It is very urgent' Vicky said. They prepared Hot Tea. He drank it and thanked the villagers and left for the caves.

What he had dreamt many a times now became a reality.

Every step he took was a burden. The soft snow beneath his feet was getting increasingly deeper. Vicky stood still and looked around. The rising Moon was chasing the setting Sun. All he could hear was the ghastly wind piping through the hills and his own unabated breath. If he did not make it to a shelter before the night fall, he thought, he will suffer from exhaustion, frost bite and hunger.

When Man loses hope on everything else, his hope on God gets stronger. When Mind sees no alternative, it ceases all other thoughts, all other emotions, all other distractions and all such scattered forces assimilate into a pointed ray of light, throwing up a cry of the soul to the Divine. With silent prayer on his lips, he kept on walking until he saw light emanating from a cave at a distance.

As he walked towards the cave, the exhaustion went away miraculously. As he approached the cave, he could hear a reverberating sound of 'Aum'. A warm feeling enveloped him. Vicky entered the cave and saw a man sitting in meditative posture. This person had a long beard and his body was lean and firm. There was a glow around his body, especially from the top of his head. Vicky stood spell bound. The person opened his eyes and they shone like diamonds. Then, he glimpsed around the cave and the entire cave was lit up a hundred lamps. He turned to Vicky and said 'Vikram. I have been waiting for you. You have found me at last'

'O Holy one. I need your help. You are omniscient. Please help me in averting this danger to the World.'

'What I am going to tell you has been kept as a secret for thousands of years. Chintamani stone is an extremely powerful creation of Nature. The possessor of the real stone can control the nature itself and he becomes extremely powerful. Ravan had the original unbroken stone with him. He died when it broke into pieces.

All the references to this stone were systematically removed from the scriptures. Generation after generation hundreds have spent their entire lives trying to know the whereabouts of this stone.

Some believed that reciting the Chintamani stotra will help them to find the path to this stone. No one had succeeded. You were right in your understanding that what you have with you now is just an outer shell of the stone. I will take you to the place where the actual stone is. But, you must have the courage and faith to understand and believe what I am going to tell you' Chandra said.

'Sir, You are my only hope. I trust you fully'

'Five thousand years ago, when Kali Yug, the present phase began, the standards of righteousness degraded to its lowest stage. Until that time, Lord Krishna kept the stone with him. He was the only one who had the capability of handling the enormous power. When Lord Krishna decided to end his incarnation, he visited the Himalayas and made a deep underground passage several meters below. There, he invoked the force of Dhumavati and placed the stone there.

The force with which he had made the deep incision on the ground resulted in a series of earthquakes. These quakes shifted the soil base and the ground opened up and the entire river of Saraswati dried up. This is the hidden mystery of disappearance of the Great Saraswati river that flowed up to Gandhar Desa or the present day Afghanistan. Come with me.' Chandra stood up and walked out of the cave.

Pleasant smell emanated from his body. As he walked the sky suddenly turned bright and the visibility improved. After walking for a few minutes, Chandra stood before a small hillock and closed his eyes. The front of the hillock cracked and bright light emerged from inside. Without saying a word, Vicky followed Chandra as he walked down the steps untouched for thousands of years.

CHAPTER : FIFTY SEVEN

The steps seemed to go down endlessly. Below a blinding light lit the entire cave. After what seemed to be an hour, they came face to face with the Chintamani stone.

The stone looked like a thousand fluorescent bulbs glowing at once. It was a blinding white light with greenish tint. Vicky could not look at it. Chandra turned back and placed his hand on Vicky's head. A strong flow of current passed through his body. His body became so light and all the fears in him vanished.

The stone remained there suspended in the air. On six corners, Vicky found extremely dark colored spheres. These huge black spheres were on the top and bottom of the stone.

'Vikram, This is the actual Chintamani stone, the search of hundreds of cults and secret societies in the past and in today's world. The actual stone is just a fistful. What you are seeing is the halo of the stone that is emanating immense brightness. The black spheres you see are controlling the stone and keeping its withholding it in all the directions. These spheres were invoked with the power of Dhumavati, the power that halts and delimits'

'What should I do now sir? I need your guidance'

'Using my power of Sadhana of Dhumavati, one of the dimension or form of Sri Maha Vidyas, I am going to place the Chintamani in a casket. But the power of this casket will drain in 54 hours from the time I place the stone in it.' Chandra closed his eyes and stretched his hand. A casket appeared on his palm.

'Now, I have to break the cage of Negative force and place the stone in this casket. Close your eyes and do not open them until I say so. If not, you will go blind.'

Vicky heard an ear bursting sound of an explosion. Yet, he did not open his eyes. After a few moments, Chandra asked him to open his eyes. The place was empty. He had a large black color casket in his hands. He approached Vicky and placed the casket on his hands. It was very heavy.

'I warn you. Do not open this casket under any circumstances. You must take this now as quickly as possible and send it to outer space in the opposite direction of the Sun. It must be done in 54 hours from now'

Vicky took the casket. It felt extremely heavy. Then Chandra closed his eyes and produced a Gold chain and he put the Talisman which Vishwa Dharma had given to Vicky and also added another Talisman.

'You will need this as well Vikram. You are not aware but you had a Brain tumor. When you touched the Chintamani piece for the first time, the healing process started. However, as you did not have the stone with you, your cancer cells started growing again. I have cured your cancer by placing my hand on you head'

He put it around Vicky's neck and said

'You are a pious and good person Vikram. My Guru had given you the talisman containing the power of Lord Shiva. I have added the power of Mother Goddess. As long as this chain is with you, you will be invincible. Nothing will stop you now. You will never feel depressed in your entire life. You now have super human capabilities and faculties. Use them for the good of humanity'

Vicky felt his strength grow a hundred times. He and Chandra walked up the stairs. Vicky bowed to the Holy Chandra and walked down briskly towards the village. He made his way back in half the time.

He spotted two choppers. Vicky was ecstatic. As he rushed towards the place, Lisa ran towards him and gave him a hug. After a brief exchange of words, they got down to business at hand.

The Indian Government had first contemplated sending out the stone into the space from Sri Hari Kota, the satellite launching coastal town in Andhra Pradesh, which was north of Chennai. Better known as SHAR or Sri Hari Kota Range, it was the pivotal satellite launch pad in South Asia. People believe that the presence of Changalamma temple and the presence of abundant Thorium in the soil made SHAR as successful and as famous as it is.

Unfortunately, SHAR could not deploy the shuttle. Indian Space Research Organization or ISRO needed at least four days time to set this. This agency had recently sent a Mars probe at a fraction of what NASA spent.

The only alternative left was NASA's emergency space shuttle vehicle and rocket which could be deployed in 20 hours at Cape Canaveral, Florida.

CHAPTER: FIFTY EIGHT

Twenty four hours ago, an elderly soft spoken Korean Gentleman faced the Indian Immigration officer. The officer asked him some questions and stamped his passport, officially letting the incognito Lee Hung into the Indian Territory.

That night Lee received a vital input on his Satellite phone. He checked-out of the Hotel and went back to the Airport. New Delhi Airport is considered as one of the best in the world. The world class facilities an efficiency with which the airport is run had won many admirers.

Lee purchased a domestic route ticket and waited patiently at the departure lounge. He loitered around the gates and identified an Airport Personnel from North East India who resembled him in physique and features. The hapless janitor walked into the washroom. His body would be found after 5 hours in a badly mutilated manner shoved into a toilet.

Lee walked freely along the building shade facing the taxiway and the tarmac. He waited patiently for further instructions. All he wanted now is the information on Vicky's flight.

When Vicky and Lisa landed in Delhi, a person from the American Embassy was waiting for them with escort them to a private jet to JFK. 'There is a plane on the stand by. We do not have much time'

'Alpha-Queen on the double' he instructed the chauffeur as he slammed the door of the Limo that would take them straight to the Business Jet chartered for them.

'Lisa we have only 40 hours to go' Vicky reminded her. He got a tense face as a reply from her. Life had come full circle for Vicky. Just a few weeks back, he was traveling to JFK on Coach class. His importance to this world was minuscule. Today, he was on the verge of avoiding a global disaster.

Meanwhile at the Falcon Jet, the cabin crew were awaiting the VIP passengers. The take off was smooth. Lisa had secured the box in the overhead cabin. She was tired and dozed off.

Then it happened. She heard a loud thud and a shriek. She saw Vicky holding legs of a familiar looking guy and hitting his body against the fuselage frame.

It was all over in a few moments. Later she would learn how Lee Hung came and try to apply Hwarang Ho and how Vicky gave him a death blow with his Kaliri Payattu, the ancient Indian martial art and kill Lee in a violent manner with his bare hands.

They landed at JFK and immediately flew to Florida and from the airport to the launch site at Cape Canaveral by a chopper.

They had only a few hours before the Space Administration officials can secure the Casket and place it into a pressurized container with mega plastic explosives. Once this was done, the countdown began. Vicky checked his watch. If the launch sequence went good, then he had succeeded.

In Washington DC, in Langley, VA and in FBI Head Quarters and in the meeting room of the launch site, everyone's eyes were glued to the monitors as the countdown began. The lift off went on smoothly. After a few minutes, Cape Canaveral reported the mission as a success. The container was rocketed thousands of miles into the space and it was blown into bits. From Earth below, it just looked like a flash of light.

CHAPTER: FIFTY NINE

Thousands of miles across in Yongbyan, the scientists reported to their Leader that the stone had stopped working. When they checked it, it looked like just a piece of glass.

Kim Jong-un was sleeping when he received a phone call. He woke up, went on to take a shower, cleansing his body thoroughly and called for a meeting of his trusted aides.

'I want 120 dogs to severely starve' he roared 'The traitor will be fed to them'. Next day Kim-Jong-un's Uncle, Jang Song-thaek and five officials were arrested. Two days later in one of the most horrifying punishment ever meted out to anyone, he and the five officials were stripped naked and fed to the 120 hungry hounds while hundreds of North Korean officers watched along with their leader. For the North Korean leader, any failure must be the handiwork of a traitor and he must be punished severely.

Vicky was invited to the White House and the President gave him a Commendation and a Shield of Honor. It was a very low key affair at the Oval office. The entire episode of the Chintamani stone was kept 'Classified' and out of access.

'We thank you personally and your Great country for what you have achieved today. Certainly, without the ancient wisdom of your Great Civilization, the world would have been a different place today.'

That was a remarkable day in Vicky's life.

Vicky was offered a visiting faculty position and an Honorary PhD by Rixton University. He was given a full time position, which he cordially declined. He said that the treasure trove of knowledge was in India. If Noetic Science has to progress and if Science were to evolve, Humans must strengthen their faculties to perceive what is not obvious to the naked eye.

Vicky was asked to say a few words after receiving the Ph.D.

'India and its great religion of Hinduism have given the world its wonderful fragrance of Saffron. The Saffron color which is worn by our Holy men is a color of Peace. It also is the color of enlightenment. Wherever the Hindus went throughout the world—thousands of years before Columbus was born—they carried this message. They also carried with them a great condiment of Saffron Grass which they used in the food offered to the Gods. Saffron Grass and the Saffron color may not be overtly visible. But the essence and the flavor of the religion is deeply rooted in every civilization of our Humanity. That is the significance of my country and my religion'.

Vicky met Rachana. She found it difficult to believe what Vicky had said about the holy man in the cave and how he had detected the brain tumor and cured it. She ran more tests and was awe-struck to find no trace of any tumor.

'I wish we had the Chintamani stone with us. It would have helped Humanity to find solutions to Cancer and related life-threatening diseases' she rued.

'It has guided us. It has shown us the direction which will someday give us the solutions Rachana. We must focus on spontaneous remission and study how the sick cells start healing as a result of strong positive suggestive thoughts an energy this generated because of this. Spontaneous regression is the key. I am going back to India. I will focus on this subject'

CHAPTER: SIXTY

The word 'Noetic' comes from the Greek word 'Nous' and it means 'Mind'

Institute of Noetic Studies was founded in the United States by Paul Temple and a former astronaut Edgar Mitchell. The campus at Petaluma, California has a resort and full-fledged research facilities. This has been running since 1973.

Owing to its nature, Noetic science is ideally inclined for research in India. Indian ancient seers had mastered this and they were able to influence the outcomes in Nature. They had brought the discursive mind under control and reaped its potential. They had mastered Nature and were able to perform supernatural feats.

As technology portends to increasingly converge with intuitive aspect of everyday life, study of Noetic science and application of its framework and dynamics will result in a paradigm shift in scientific research.

With proper focus and deeper understanding of the ancient wisdom and the knowledge and tools that are at disposal, in a few decades humans will become very powerful, as they will then have the ability not only to make their present times better, but also make their future predictable and manageable.

This synergy will catapult humanity to a species of higher ability and potential. In the story of evolution, this will propel Homo-Sapiens to move towards being a better species. Chintamani stone is just an object. Its greatness lies in its properties. These properties can be adopted by the human mind and when it happens, we become divine.

A week later, Vicky was back in Chennai. His two friends were ready to test their motorcycle riding skills. Vicky was not nervous anymore and he did not have a Pepsi can in his hand. Instead, he had a packet of Tropicana Orange Juice.

'Eh, look at our realized soul' Ravi teased looking at Vicky.

'Now, for your information, Tropicana is a brand owned by PepsiCo' Vicky laughed. 'The word 'Orange' came from India. Its roots are from the word 'Naranj'. Europeans did not what to call the Orange color and they adopted it. You will be also proud to know that the world

'Citrus' also came from India. It came from 'Santara' which is the Hindi name for the Orange fruit.'

'Okay Master. This is not a classroom. Let's race' cried Ravi.

That day for the first time in his life, he won the race. He won by 54 seconds. It was a clear improvement by 108 seconds.

But, is there an End to the Human spirit?

Jayanti te sukrutino rasa siddhaaha kaveesvaraaha

Naasti teshaam yasah kaaye jaraa maranajam bhayam

An accomplished author, who had written a great work, does not fear death due to illness or accident.